James T

DARCY LANE

AUSTIN MACAULEY PUBLISHERS™

LONDON • CAMBRIDGE • NEW YORK • SHARJAH

A CIP catalogue record for this title is available from the British Library.

ISBN 9781398400177 (Paperback)
ISBN 9781398400184 (ePub e-book)

www.austinmacauley.com

First Published (2020)
Austin Macauley Publishers Ltd
25 Canada Square
Canary Wharf
London
E14 5LQ

Chapter 1
White Violet

Lancashire, England

Sat under a dusty roof, Elise, a petite girl with daisy blonde hair sat reading alone in her bed. The room in which she lay was barren; her bed was made from a metal that moaned when she moved, and the floor was old and worn. The wallpaper was cracked and tired, its flaws visible against the light from her bedside lamp. On the floor lay scattered toys, perhaps the only reminder of what a seven-year-old's bedroom should look like. The toys were old and well-used, having been worn and enjoyed by fragile hands.

She read quietly from her book until she heard rumblings from outside her bedroom door. She lifted her head and glanced anxiously towards the door, she waited as the noises quietened and then continued with her book. She read through the pages and paused at words she could not understand, 'Cur-curiosity,' she said to herself.

She read until her eyes became strained. She was tired and in need of sleep. She placed her book to the side, turned off her bedside lamp and rolled over into bed. She curled her pillow under her head and closed her eyes. Elise's bed sat pushed against the back wall of the room, with a small signature etched onto the frame, *Property of Elise Rose*, it read in wayward scribbles. She turned and jostled for comfort.

'Put it down!' said a voice from outside her bedroom door. 'You need to be quiet. You'll wake Elise, you dickhead.'

The voice was waning and filled with desperation. It was a familiar sound. It was the voice of Elise's mother, Grace

Rose, who had been sat in the front room with a friend for the past two hours. This was a common occurrence in Flat 31, the home Elise shared with her mother. Grace would often arrive back with a friend and Elise would often take refuge in her room. She would hide behind books and covers, while her mother enjoyed the company of others. It had become the norm.

'Fuck Elise,' said another voice.

The voice was hollow and inexplicably spiteful. 'Do you think I care? Do you really think I want to talk about your daughter?' the voice continued.

Elise and Grace had moved into the flat three years ago, when Elise was four, and her memories had just started to form and consolidate. They moved to the estate to be closer to Emmett Rose, a hunch of a man, small and stocky with greying hair. Emmett was father to Grace and grandfather to Elise. Grace had lost her job as a cleaner at the local warehouse and Emmett had promised to help her on the condition that she moved closer to home. Emmett adored Grace, but his trust with her was waning. He sold the idea as, "helping her get back on her feet", but in truth, he wanted her close so that he could watch over her and make sure that Elise was safe.

The estate was a blend of concrete blocks and stray green patches. It was cold, but warm in the summers, when Elise would run and spend time outside. She often remembered these days, long before the nights with strangers, and back when her mother was able to look her in the eye. The days were quick and bright, simple days that left warming memories of a mother she had not seen in some time.

After moving back to the estate, Grace started work at her father's shop. He owned a store selling electrical appliances, as well as tools and paint. Grace was okay for the first six months, but then her time at the shop started to wane. Emmett, a proud father had heard whispers about his daughter. Grace was a natural beauty, with daisy blonde hair, golden eyes and spring lips. As a result, hiding her indiscretions was difficult.

Emmett would often hear, 'Yeah, Emmett's daughter. The one with the face and the troubles.'

Grace's beauty had remained the same over time. Despite the long nights and short days, she had managed to keep the best parts of herself. The estate had also remained the same. The sights from the windows were the same, the shouts from the locals were still volatile and stressed, and the people there were still often misunderstood.

In the past, Flat 31 often felt like a refuge from the sometimes-unforgiving estate. Even if Elise loved to run and see the sun, she was often forced inside. However, in the past year, any peace lay outside the home. In the streets, amongst the concrete, far away from the shouting outside the door.

'Let's put some music on, none of that miserable shite you usually listen to. Something with a bit of life.'

'It's too late for music. Sit down. Stop dancing.'

'Come on!'

'Elise has school in the morning. She needs to be up early.'

'Ah, fuck Elise.'

'You're drunk.'

'This is what pisses me off. This is why I don't come round.'

The home Elise shared with her mother was minute, only the essentials were accounted for. In past years, the flat was always well-maintained. Despite her troubles, Grace took pride in her home. The walls were covered in fresh paint and the plants sat beside each other, bathing in natural light. The largest wall in the front room was painted with a soft cream colour. And, on the walls, hanging by nails, sat pictures of art and scribbles, that although not cohesive, showed a home that was cared for. Around the flat sat pictures of Grace and Elise together. Pictures of a smiling family, at days out to the beach and theme park. There were also pictures of Emmett. He stood in the pictures, pulling the girls into his seasoned frame. Grace also had talents. She made furniture, tables and chairs that she made by hand and decorated with a passion that brought life to the room. She made small stands, and even pottery. However, much of the furniture had broken, and while Elise carried no guilt, this saddened Grace deeply. The walls, too, had cracked; the once fresh paint had aged and the pictures of days out as a family had started to evoke feelings of regret rather than happiness.

Elise led curled under blankets. The feeling of the cover pulled over her head, although uncomfortable, gave a naïve sense of security, and even the possibility of sleep. She was careful about her movements; any sudden change would unsettle the frame of the bed and perhaps be heard from outside the door.

She tucked her knees into her chest and dug her feet into the mattress. As she rested, the noises from outside the door seemed to quieten. She could still hear her mother's conversation, but it was relaxed and unthreatening. She stayed quiet. She made an effort to stay as still as possible but sleep still evaded her. She pulled back her covers and looked towards her bedroom door. Silence persisted. She rested. She closed her eyes and let her mind loosen. She rested long enough to fall asleep, until she was woken by frantic screams.

'I told you to stop speaking about her!' said a voice. 'How many times have I told you. Let's see, shall we. Let's see what all the fuss is about.'

Elise woke to a struggle outside her bedroom door. She pulled back the covers and sat up in anticipation. She pushed backwards in bed and heard desperate pleas from her mother: 'Don't go in there,' she said. 'I won't mention her again, I promise. Just come and sit down.'

Elise pushed back against her headboard and the metal pushed uncomfortably against her skin.

'Come and sit down,' continued her mother's voice. 'You're drunk. You'll regret this is in the morning.'

From outside her bedroom door, she could hear her mother fighting with her friend. She slapped and pushed against his torso, but her actions lacked conviction and she was easily pushed aside. The man was losing balance. He pressed his hand against the handle and opened Elise's bedroom door. She immediately stood from her bed. Her feet were exposed against the floor and her body was struck by the cold. The man walked into her room and stumbled towards her.

'Elise!' he said. 'I didn't wake you, did I? Shouldn't you be sleeping? You have school in the morning!'

The man was pale, with a wide frame and had holes around the knees of his jeans. He walked towards her and took her by the arm. She struggled with him, but he persisted in his efforts. She tried to bite the man's hand, but he took it away and pulled her into his frame.

'So, this is Elise,' he said. 'She is pretty, I'll give you that.'

Grace stood at the door, arguing with the man. 'Michael, you're drunk. Come back out here. Please, here, have a cigarette,' she said.

'Elise don't be scared. He's only playing,' she continued.

The man took Elise into the front room. Grace hit him as he passed but he paid little attention. The front room was torn. Empty cans, bottles, discarded cigarettes butts and empty packets of food lay mingled between the furniture. Elise was pulled across the room and left near the television.

He knelt beside her: 'You're all I ever hear about. What about me, eh?'

'I think you're all she cares about.'

From behind the man, Grace took a vase and smashed it over his head. He fell from his knees and onto his hands, seemingly shocked by the act. He turned towards Grace, grabbed her, and pushed her to the floor. He began hitting her, lowering his fist into her mouth and jaw. He pulled up her top and began hitting her in the ribs, exposing old bruises around her stomach. Elise had started to cry. She rushed towards the man and hit him, but he pushed her away with ease. Grace gagged with the pain, eventually folding her head into the man's lap, and closing her eyes. The man soon stopped. He stood and sucked on his knuckles, wincing as he curled and uncurled his fingers. Elise nudged away from him. He was swaying and talking from under his breath.

He turned and looked towards her: 'Here we are. Come here, will you?'

Elise tried to move towards the front door, but her actions lacked confidence and an outstretched arm was enough to stop her.

'Don't fucking try it,' he said. 'Stay exactly where you are.'

The man slumbered to the side of the room and took a stray bottle of vodka from the floor. He closed his eyes and pushed the bottle towards his lips. He straddled the bottle as he walked towards her. He knelt beside her and once again took her by the arm.

'I'm Michael,' he said. 'I don't think we've met. I'm friends with your mum.'

From over his shoulder, Elise could see her mother moving on the floor.

'Don't worry about her,' he said. 'She's just resting.'

Grace stood and stabbed the man in the neck with a shard from the broken vase. The man held his hand to his neck and found blood running over his skin. He turned towards Grace. She tried to run away, but he took her by the arm. He rummaged in his pocket and took out a small knife. He started to stab Grace repeatedly. He stabbed her in the lungs and arm.

Grace dropped to the floor and the man fell with her. He continued to stab her in the arms and torso. Once again, Elise rushed to her mother's aid, but once again, she was easily pushed away. She could hear the man stabbing her mother. She turned away and placed her hands over her ears.

Eventually, the sounds stopped. The man stood and walked away from Grace. Elise turned and saw blood running from open wounds. She crawled towards her mother and stayed with her until the front door was forced open by two police officers. The officers had shocked looks on their faces. They rushed into the room and took the man to the ground, pushing his head into the floor and placing handcuffs around his wrists. The police officers were closely followed by Elise's neighbour from across the hall, Olivia, a smiling woman in her mid-thirties, who spent her time raising her children and working at the local swimming baths.

Olivia rushed into the room and sweltered over Grace's stricken figure.

'No, no, no, Grace,' she said. 'Elise, are you hurt? Did he hurt you?'

Olivia took Elise in her arms and walked with her across the hallway.

'I should have called sooner!' she said. Olivia was usually a relaxed figure, but tonight her face was stretched with panic. She took Elise to her flat and placed her on top of the kitchen side: 'You have blood all over you. Fuck, fuck, I should have called sooner.'

Olivia's stare soon became damp. She was fumbling and became angered when she heard the door to her children's bedroom open.

'Stay in there!' she shouted, as her youngest boy peered his head around the door.

She touched Elise's skin. 'Are you cut?' she asked. 'Elise, are you cut?'

Elise shook her head and looked down towards her blood-soaked clothes. They were soon joined by another police officer.

'Is she hurt?' he asked.

'No, she's not hurt. I don't think so, anyway.'

'What's her name?'

'Elise. Elise Rose.'

'Elise, don't worry. You're fine. We're going to take you to the hospital, just to check you over. It's nothing to worry about. The ambulance will be here soon, okay?'

Elise nodded. From outside Olivia's flat, she could hear angered speech as the man was taken away.

'You sick bastard!' said one of the officers.

'Clear the hallway!' shouted another.

Elise nudged back and wiped her hands on her pyjama pants. She looked out towards the hallway, but Olivia stood in front of her.

'Don't look out there,' she said. 'Look at me. Keep your eyes on me.'

Olivia looked towards the police officer and grabbed him by the arm.

'I should have called sooner!' she said. 'I should have fucking called sooner!'

'Is there usually trouble?' asked the officer.

'Trouble? Yeah, there's trouble. Shouting, yes. Arguments, but never this. I never thought this would happen.'

The officer took Olivia by the side and tucked her into his frame. He stretched out a hand and touched Elise on the shoulder: 'We'll be out of here soon. You've been very brave. Just wait a little longer.'

'The ambulances are here!' shouted a voice from inside the hallway. 'The daughter first.'

'Are you coming?' asked the police officer.

'I can't,' said Olivia. 'I have the kids.'

The police officer took Elise and placed her on the floor beside him.

'Hold my hand,' he said.

Elise looked out towards the hallway. She could hear a team of medics rushing up the stairs and towards her mother. She was led from the room and out into the hallway. Her feet were still exposed against the floor and her hands were cold against the police officer's warm skin.

'Elise, I'll be at the hospital as soon as I can,' said Olivia, from behind.

She reached the hallway to see a team of medics working on her mother's frame.

'Close the fucking door!' shouted the police officer holding her hand. There was emotion in his tone and his face had reddened.

He picked her up and put her over his shoulder. Another officer, stood by the door to Flat 31, stepped inside and pulled the door shut. The officer carried Elise through the hallway and towards the stairs. She clung to the man's frame. He spoke with her as they walked down the stairs, but she did not respond.

At the bottom of the stairs, there was another team of medics. A tall man with a handsome frame held open the door while the police officer carried her from the apartment block.

About her, the night was dull. Neighbours peered from windows and she could feel the cold against her feet. She was taken and placed in the back of the first ambulance. She was met by another medic, a woman with short bobbed hair and a tired expression.

'What's her name?' she asked.

'Elise,' replied the officer. 'Elise Rose.'

The medic took Elise and began inspecting her. She turned and looked towards the front of the ambulance.

'Let's go!' she said.

'Let's go!' said the officer.

'Let's go,' said Elise, quietly.

Chapter 2
The Last Day on the Unit

Thirteen Years Later

Summer at the unit was ending and Elise was outside, enjoying the last of the morning sun before autumn returned. Elise was grown now, having recently celebrated her 20th birthday with all her friends and staff at the psychiatric unit. As years passed, Elise's face had moulded into a beauty similar to her mother's, and despite great strain, her eyes had remained golden. Her body had matured and her once youthful stare had become hardened.

She stood in the garden at the back of the unit, leaning against the entrance to the shelter. The shelter was a beloved part of the unit, a space where patients enjoyed fruitful days and warm mornings as a reward for good behaviour and progress in their rehabilitation. The shelter had been made by the staff at the unit; pieces of wood that had been nailed together and painted with whites and blues. The shelter was a place of calm, providing a chance for the patients to unwind from the monotonous corridors, therapy sessions and steel beds. The shelter was the centrepiece of the garden, and Elise's favourite place to talk and sit with friends.

Across from the shelter was a small bench, and along the walls of the garden, sat tidy green bushes with roots and waning leaves. There was a stone path leading from the shelter to the dining hall, where staff and trusted patients cleared away the day's breakfast.

Elise was joined in the shelter by Dora, her closest friend at the unit, a passionate woman with thick curly brown hair and a contagious grin.

'You must be excited,' she said, as she ran a brush through her hair. 'Your last day at the unit. How exciting. I remember when you first arrived, all scared and full of madness.'

'I'm sad to see you go,' she continued. 'We've become quite close.'

'I'm still surprised they're letting me out.'

'No, you're better. More relaxed. Anyway, you should enjoy it.'

'Yeah, but part of me will miss this place. The unit, I mean.'

The unit was quiet this morning. Elise had been allowed to visit the garden as a reward for her rehabilitation.

'You've come a long way,' said Dr Laghari, during their last session together. 'This is the right time for you to move on.'

'Am I allowed in the garden?' asked Elise. 'On my last morning?'

Dr Laghari grinned. 'Yes,' she said. 'Everyone is allowed to visit the garden on their last morning. You can take a friend too.'

Elise had chosen Dora without hesitation. Dr Laghari told Elise that she should use the rest of her time at the unit to prepare herself for leaving. She took the advice. She spent time with friends and made lists of the things she wanted to do on the outside world. It had been a peaceful last few weeks at the unit. The staff were relaxed, the hallways were quiet and there had been no incidents in some time.

Elise stepped out of the shelter and looked upwards towards the sky. She squinted. 'It doesn't feel like my last day,' she said. 'I thought I'd feel different.'

'Different, how?' asked Dora.

'I don't know. Changed? Optimistic, maybe.'

'I wouldn't get carried away,' said Dora.

'Do you think I'll be back?' asked Elise. 'Get readmitted, like Carol and Dee?'

'I don't know. Do you think you'll be back?'

'I hope not.'

'I think you'll be fine. Carol and Dee don't help themselves.'

Elise walked back towards the shelter and scratched at her tongue. She could still taste the medication. 'I still have to take medication,' she said. 'If I'm rehabilitated, why do I still need to take medication?'

'At least you'll be able to take it without somebody watching you,' replied Dora, sharply.

Elise's last day at the unit came with threats of her past life. She had been ordered to the unit by law, taken against her will and placed under the watch of trained staff. She felt mistreated at first, as though she had been taken without due cause.

'This is normal,' said one of the members of staff during her first week. 'No one feels comfortable at first. You'll feel differently in a month or so.'

The member of staff was right. After her first month, she started to adapt to the unit and grow as a patient. She even started to see similarities between herself and the other patients.

Calling her grandfather after two months at the unit, and saying, 'I feel okay here, Grandad. I think this is the best place for me.'

Elise's grandfather visited her regularly. The unit was only a short way from their home, so he came often. As well as the visits, Elise's time at the unit included regular sessions with an assigned psychiatrist. She enjoyed her sessions with Dr Laghari from the start. She was a professional woman with an unnatural ability to make her feel at ease. 'You're in a bit of a mess at the moment. I can see it on your face, but we can sort it all out. We can sort it all out together,' she said to Elise during their first meeting.

Elise liked her from the start. To supplement the therapy sessions, Elise was given a dose of medication to be taken each morning. She was told that the pills would "help her see things more clearly", but she despised them and hated taking them. She had been taking the pills every morning for just under two years, having been admitted to the unit, only a short while after her 18th birthday.

Despite this, she felt comfortable here. The predictability of the days at the unit had caused a calmness within her. Her limbs had begun to loosen, and her clarity restored. Even if her fellow patients were often unpredictable, she was happy here. However, today marked the end of that happiness and the end of her stay at the unit. She would be leaving and returning to her old life. Her last morning at the unit would soon be over and her grandfather would arrive to take her home.

After the incident in Flat 31, Elise moved with her grandfather from the estate and into a house close by. She could still see the estate from her bedroom window, but the change of home was needed. She had not been back to the estate since she was a child, and in truth, she hoped she never would.

'Come and sit down with me,' said Dora. 'This is our last morning together, after all.'

Elise moved from the entrance of the shelter and sat down next to Dora. Dora continued to brush her hair.

'Is that your brush?' asked Elise. 'I've never seen it before.'

'No,' said Dora. 'I stole it from Sue.'

'It's no good, though,' she continued. 'Do you have one I could have, now that you're leaving?'

'Yeah,' said Elise. 'There's a green one in my room. You can have that.'

'Thanks,' said Dora 'I'll give this one back to Sue then.'

'Yeah. You know how frantic she gets.'

'Oh, I nearly forgot to ask. Have you signed the wall yet?'

'What wall?' replied Elise

'The wall at the back of the shelter.'

'This shelter?'

'No, the other shelter. Of course this shelter.'

'What do you mean, sign it?'

'Everyone signs it on their last day. Did you not know? It's tradition.'

'It sounds like a stupid tradition to me.'

'You can't leave without doing it. I have a pen in my pocket. You can do it now.'

Dora stood and took a black marker pen from her pocket. She smiled and threw it onto Elise's lap.

'Everyone signs the wall,' she said. 'It's tradition!'

Dora pulled Elise by the arm. 'Stand up,' she said. 'Stand up!'

Elise stood and passed the pen to Dora. 'I'm not signing it,' she said. 'If I go on the grass, I'll ruin my shoes.'

'You're doing it!' said Dora, as she pulled her to the back of the shelter.

Elise fought with her, but Dora was much stronger. 'Get off me!' she said. 'I'm not signing your stupid wall!'

Dora took her to the back of the shelter and pointed towards the window. 'Go on, then,' she said. 'Climb through.'

'Through what?'

'The window.'

'Why would I climb through the window?'

'Alright then. I'll go first, but you're next.'

Dora used her arms to push herself up. She slumbered over the window and landed on the rain-soaked grass.

'It was raining last night!' said Elise. 'You're going to ruin your shoes.'

Dora looked towards her feet. Her shoes were covered in splashes of mud. 'I'll swap them later,' she said. 'Beth's always leaving her shoes about. We're the same size.'

Elise smiled and shook her head. She was laughing until she heard the door to the dining hall open behind her. She turned to find a member of staff walking towards her.

'Fuck, this is your fault. We're going to get in trouble,' she said.

Dora turned in the mud: 'Why do you care, you're leaving. Surely this is your time to misbehave?'

'I don't want them thinking bad of me,' said Elise. 'Not on my last day.'

Elise watched as the man neared the shelter. He was a recognisable member of staff. He had a wide frame and narrow features. He walked along the path as though it was a burden. With his face wearing a faint grimace. He arrived at the shelter slightly out of breath. He stopped by the entrance.

'Elise,' he began. 'Isn't it your last day?'

Elise smiled. 'Yes,' she said. 'My grandad will be here soon. Sorry about Dora, she's just messing about.'

The man pointed towards the back wall of the shelter. 'Well, you can't leave without signing the wall,' he said. 'So, you better get to it.'

Elise blushed, 'Not you as well. So, you want me to climb through the window and ruin my shoes?'

'Don't worry about your shoes,' said the man. 'Sign the wall. It's tradition!'

'I've been telling her,' said Dora, with a smirk on her face.

The man grinned and started walking back along the path. 'Tradition!' he said as he walked.

Dora stood, childishly smiling at Elise. 'Come on,' she said. 'Climb through.'

Elise climbed through the window and stepped out onto the grass. 'My shoes!' she continued.

She followed Dora to the back of the shelter and stood in front of the wall. She was struck by the masses of signatures and farewell messages.

'You might struggle for a place,' said Dora. 'The wall's nearly full. There's been so many people. It's hard to remember them all.'

Elise rolled the pen in her hands and settled on a place in the bottom left corner. She knelt and scribbled her name. *Elise Rose room 4*, she wrote.

She stood and passed the pen back to Dora. 'Happy?' she asked.

'Happy,' replied Dora with a smile on her face.

They left the wall and returned to the shelter. Elise walked across the grass and through the entrance, while Dora climbed back through the window.

'You can leave now,' she said. 'Your time's been served.'

Elise sat with Dora until she was called by a loud shout. 'Elise Rose!' shouted a member of staff from the dining hall. 'Time to go. Your grandad's here!'

Elise instantly became panicked. Her hands started to sweat and her breath became short.

'It feels strange,' she said, 'just leaving.'

Dora snarled and pushed her away. 'Be good,' she said. 'I'll see you soon!'

'I'll see you soon,' said Elise. 'And make sure you give Sue her brush back.'

Elise embraced Dora for a final time and then started walking towards reception. She followed the member of staff through the corridors and towards her grandfather. She walked into reception to find her grandfather smiling and holding a small bottle of water. She walked towards him and hugged him.

'I thought you might want some water,' he said. 'It's hot outside.'

Emmett took Elise by the arms. 'You look well,' he said. 'Taller, as well.'

'I've already signed you out,' he continued. 'I have your medication too.'

'So, we can go?'

'I'm not sure.'

All the necessary procedures were then taken care of. Elise had a brief chat with Dr Laghari, who gave her a quick reminder about her medication schedule. She then left the unit with her grandfather. They rushed to the car and put on their seatbelts. Both smiling at one another. The drive home was quick. Emmett asked questions and Elise answered where possible. As they drove, Elise became increasingly unnerved. They drove home, past small shops and children on bikes. They drove until they reached Hirst Street.

'44,' said Emmett. 'Home.'

As they stopped outside 44 Hirst Street, Elise became tense. She was unsure if this was the start of something new or the continuation of something old and troublesome. She undid her seat belt with deep uncertainty.

'So,' said Emmett. 'You're all sorted?'

Elise simply smiled and left the car. She followed her grandfather inside the house. Inside, Emmett threw down his coat and walked towards the kitchen. 'I have some bad news,' he said.

'What?' asked Elise.

'Some pricks burgled the store a few weeks ago. I didn't want to trouble you, but I thought you should know.'

'Really? Have you told the police?'

'Yeah, they think they'll catch them. Plenty of evidence, they said.'

'What did they take, the pricks?'

'Tools, money. They had their fun, put it that way, but it's nothing to worry about. It will all be sorted soon. Tea?'

'No, thanks.'

She left her grandad and returned to her bedroom for the first time in nearly two years. She was happy to see that it had not changed. She sat on her bed and felt happy to be home. Perhaps, it was the start of something new. She rested on her bed until she heard sombre sounds from outside her window. She stood and moved towards the sounds. From outside her window, she could see a boy sitting on the wall at the back of her house. She opened the window and shouted towards him, 'Get off my wall, you scumbag!' she said.

The boy turned and grinned. 'Elise!' he said. 'When did you get back?'

'Just now, about ten minutes ago.'

'Let you out then, did they?'

'Yeah.'

'I'll warn the locals, shall I? Sound the alarm?' he said, 'Come down, anyway. You can tell me all about it.'

The boy's name was Tom Jacks. He had been Elise's neighbour since she moved to the house with her grandfather. He was young and unambitious. She joined him on the wall.

'It's the second time I've had to climb today,' she said. 'I was hoping for a peaceful day.'

She started to tell him about her time at the unit.

'You should've visited me,' she said.

Tom titled his head, 'I was going to, but I thought you might want your space.'

'I was there for nearly two years!' said Elise sharply.

Tom nodded and looked out. The view from the wall was familiar. They had seen it all their lives; concrete tarnished by sprays of graffiti and discarded cigarette butts. Tom scratched at the side of his head. 'You've been gone a long time,' he said. 'It's strange to be sitting next to you.'

'I guess people have been talking,' she said.

'I wouldn't know.'

'Still lonely, are you?'

'No, just happy in my own company.'

'And mine.'

'Yeah, and yours.'

'Ha-ha.'

Tom clapped his hands together and stretched his arms out towards the concrete. 'You're back!' he said.

She smiled. 'So, any news?' she asked.

'Miss. Lambert died,' said Tom.

'What? The lady from down the street?'

'Yeah.'

'Ah, I always liked her.'

'I thought she was a bit of a bitch, honestly.'

'Tom.'

'Well, you know.'

'So, no news apart from that?'

'Actually,' said Tom. 'There is something. I have something for you.'

'What is it?'

'A journal.'

'A journal? Whose journal?'

'Your mum's. A woman came round looking for you. She asked me to give it you when I next saw you.'

'Have you read it?'

'No, why would I?'

'What else did she say, this woman?'

He jumped from the wall, 'She said she was friends with your mum.'

Elise watched as Tom started walking back towards his house. 'Where are you going?' she asked.

He pinched his face. 'To get it,' he said. 'I presume you want it?'

Elise stuttered. 'It's just a bit of a surprise,' she said.

Tom smiled widely. 'It might be a good surprise,' he said. 'Wait here. I'll go and get it.'

Chapter 3
The Phonebox

The Phonebox was discrete, hidden behind alleys and streets, it lay on the periphery of town life. The Phonebox was a place of solace, rarely seen by the eye and rarely heard in conversations around town. The Phonebox was hard to find. It sat just outside the town centre and was marked by an old red telephone box.

Elise and Tom walked purposefully through the streets.

'So, you've not been in two years?' he asked. 'You must've missed it.'

She turned the corner and kicked a small stone towards the road. 'Just less than two years, actually,' she said. 'And yeah, I have. I hope it's not changed.'

They crossed the road together. Elise scurried nervously, and Tom strolled as though he carried little weight.

'It's not changed,' he said. 'I was there a few months ago when there was a karaoke night. It still looks the same to me.'

'It's around here somewhere,' she said. 'It's up there, isn't it?'

'Can you not remember where it is?'

'Yeah I can.'

'Well, I know where it is,'

'Let me try and find it.'

'Okay, but don't get us lost.'

The Phonebox found character in privacy. It was less a secret and more a refuge from the stretching arm of the busier, more bustling town centre. He shoved his hands in his pockets and glanced nervously towards her. 'Are you sure you know the way?' he asked.

They walked until they reached Cobham Road. 'It's here!' she said. 'Cobham Road.'

They crossed the street and Elise smiled. 'I told you I knew where it was,' she said.

Across the street there was an old red telephone box. It sat just inside a small alleyway. The telephone box was ragged, seemingly marred by the streets around it. She stretched out and touched it. 'It still needs to be painted,' she said. 'Is it still broken?'

'Probably,' said Tom. 'I've never seen anyone use it, anyway.'

The sight of the telephone box created an excitement within her. She smiled and small creases formed around her eyes. 'Should we go in?' she asked. 'I could do with a drink.'

The alleyway leading towards The Phonebox was narrow. They stepped through the pools of water and stray cigarette butts until they reached a small set of stairs. The stairs led to a set of doors. The doors were naked; no signs hung, no offers, no deals, or incentives to come inside, but they stepped inside without hesitation.

The Phonebox was warm against the cold outside. It was quiet too, with only a smattering of people sat amongst the tables and chairs. At the front of The Phonebox, there was an old man sat at a small table, reading from the newspaper. Elise remembered him. He was a regular here before she was sent away. He had not changed at all, which, to Elise, was a welcome sight. She walked past the man and towards the bar. The bar was watched over by a younger man, who stood, leaning against the back of the bar, reading from a book. The man heard Elise's footsteps, lifted his head, and made a small fold in his page. He placed his book to the side and greeted her with an unusual smile. 'What can I get you?' he asked. 'Still gin, is it?'

Elise smiled, 'You remember?'

'Yeah, I remember. Still eighteen, are you?'

'Yeah still eighteen.'

'Good. No problem, then.'

'Beer for me,' said Tom. 'Any will do.'

The barman made their drinks and placed two glasses in front of them. 'Seven pounds,' he said.

They swapped spare change with the barman and took their drinks. They chose to sit at a table in the far corner of the room. They slumbered to their chairs and placed their glasses on the table. The barman then returned to reading his book at the back of the bar.

She sat and looked around. 'You're right,' she said. 'It's the same as I remember.'

The Phonebox could be described as antique. It had a dark wooden floor, no windows, no natural light, and pictures of telephone boxes on the walls. Opposite them, in the corner of the room, sat another red telephone box. However, this one was new and pristine, with a small sign hanging on the door that read, *free calls*.

She sat and drank from above her bottom lip. The taste of the gin warmed her senses and she started to relax. 'It's a pleasure to be back,' she said. 'This is my first drink in two years. I'll probably be falling over after it.'

As they sat, The Phonebox became busier and busier.

'I prefer it when it's quiet,' she said.

'It's Saturday,' replied Tom, as he read from the newspaper.

Elise acquired more gin and sat drinking throughout the afternoon. She was happy until she got the unusual feeling that she was being watched. From across the room, she could see three men talking and looking in her direction. She took a quick sip and nudged Tom on the arm, 'Those men are looking at me,' she said.

'That didn't take long,' he replied. 'If they ask to buy you a drink, tell them to get me one as well.'

'No, they're actually looking at me.'

'Where?'

'Over there, at that table.'

'Oh yeah, they are looking at you.' A pause. 'Well, they're looking at both of us now.'

'Go and tell them to stop.'

'Oh yeah, I'll just go over and tell them.'

'Go on.'

'Just look away. They'll stop eventually.'

She blushed. 'What's their problem?' she asked.

Tom glanced back towards the men, 'They weren't at the unit with you, were they?'

Elise scowled, 'No they weren't, prick.'

'That one at the back looks like he could've been. The one with the beady eyes.'

Elise sat up in her chair. 'They're coming over,' she said. 'Sit up, they're coming over.'

The three men had stood and started walking towards them. She was nervous until she recognised one of the men. 'Elise!' he said. 'Do you remember me?'

Elise stood to greet the man. It was Elijah Jones, an old friend from the estate. He was a tumultuous boy, built with enthusiasm.

'Elijah,' she said. 'You look different.'

'Well, I'd hope so,' he replied. 'I thought you were still in hospital.'

'No, I just got out.'

'Climbed through the window, did you?'

'Funny.'

'Anyway, there's someone I want you to meet. This is Jack Clapham. He was friends with your mum. Jack, this is Elise.'

Elise looked at Jack and felt an unusual feeling in her hands. There was something different about him from the start. He was well dressed, with a slim frame and an unusually heavy stare. He held out his hand and greeted her.

'I'm Jack,' he said. 'I was friends with your mum.'

Beside Jack was another man. 'This is Frankie,' said Jack. 'Don't be scared. He's not the friendliest.'

Frankie was slim like Jack, with short greying hair. He watched Elise carefully. 'Nice to meet you,' he said. 'I'm Frankie.'

Elijah was buoyant. 'How's Emmett?' he asked.

'Good,' said Elise. 'The shop got burgled, but he's good. How's your mum?'

'Yeah same old. Still not happy with me. More wrinkles these days, as well.'

As Elise spoke with Elijah, she could feel Jack watching her. He was taller than her and she could feel him above her. 'You look so much like your mum,' he said eventually. 'It's like standing right next to her.'

Elise stuttered. 'How did you know her?' she asked.

'We lived across the street from each other, growing up,' replied Jack. 'We were good friends. I know your grandad too. Emmett.'

Elise looked toward Elijah, 'How do you two know each other?'

'Jack's just helping me out,' said Elijah.

'I live with him,' he continued. 'My mum kicked me out. I work at his shop too. He owns a garage across town.'

'Your mum kicked you out?'

'Yeah, she's sick of the trouble. For the best, really.'

'Elijah was telling me that you've been in hospital.' said Jack.

'Yeah,' she said.

'Quick drink to celebrate?'

'No, not exactly. This is Tom, by the way. He lives next door to me.'

Jack stretched out an arm and greeted Tom, 'All right,' he said.

'All right,' replied Tom.

Jack seemed enthused. He was smiling irrationally and rarely took his eyes away from Elise. 'How long were you in hospital for?' he asked. 'If you don't mind me asking.'

'Two years. Well, nearly two years.'

'That's a long time.'

'Yeah, long.'

'You'll need some help getting back on your feet.'

'Will I?'

'Everyone needs help.'

'Help with what?'

'Whatever.'

'I'm all good for help, thanks.'

'Okay, well, I just thought I'd come over and say hello, we have to get going now,' continued Jack. 'But take my number. Call if you ever need anything.'

Elise took a scrap of paper from Jack and placed it in her pocket. 'Do you always carry your number around with you?' she asked.

Jack laughed, 'No, not always. It must be your lucky day.' He smiled again and stepped back. 'Anyway,' he said. 'We need to go.'

Jack nodded at Tom and smiled at Elise for a final time. His smile was wide and white. 'I'll see you,' he said. 'Don't be afraid to call.'

He turned and started walking from the bar. Frankie followed behind him, avoiding eye contact with Elise, and talking angrily with Jack.

Elijah paused before leaving. 'He can help you,' he said. 'Jack, I mean. Be sure to call him if you ever need anything.'

Elise nodded. 'I'll keep it in mind,' she said. 'See you, Elijah. Stay out of trouble.'

Elijah then followed the two men from the bar. As they left, Tom sat up in his chair. 'What the fuck was that?' he asked.

Elise sat back down. 'What?' she asked.

'That guy. Who was he?'

'Jack,' she replied. 'He just told us he was called Jack.'

'That was a bit weird, don't you think? Call if you need anything. You hardly know him.'

'I don't know him.'

'He seemed to know you. He seemed to know you very well.'

'He was friends with my mum.'

'You don't know that.'

'He's not going to lie, is he? Why would he?'

'It's just a bit strange. That's all I'm saying.'

'Ah, don't worry about it.'

As the afternoon passed, Elise and Tom left The Phonebox. Tom was eager to get home.

'How are we getting home?' he asked. 'I'm not walking.'

Elise shrugged. She did not share his ambition to return home. 'I don't want to go home,' she said. 'Let's find something new. Something different.'

Tom laughed and pulled her into his frame. 'There's nothing new round here,' he said.

'Home time,' he continued. 'Come on, we'll get the bus.'

They walked the streets and stopped at the closest bus stop. Elise stood while Tom sat.

'Ah,' she continued. 'I don't want to go home. Stop being a bore.'

Tom ignored her. He stood when he saw the number 12 bus coming towards him. 'We'll get this,' he said. 'It'll take us close enough.'

The bus stopped, and they got on. They paid the bus driver and sat down at the back of the bus. Elise looked from the window while Tom wiped at a small stain on his jeans. As she sat, the thought of returning home saddened her. The bus moved through the streets, past wild children, and other pedestrians.

Tom coughed and crossed one leg over the other. 'I'm still thinking about that man,' he said. 'Jack Clapham.'

Elise turned and looked towards him. 'Forget him,' she said. 'We'll probably never see him again.'

Soon, the bus stopped near Hirst Street. Tom stood and gestured to leave. 'Come on,' he said, 'this is us.'

'I don't want to go home,' said Elise.

'But this is our stop.'

'I'm staying.'

'Why?'

'Because I don't want to go home.'

'Are you actually staying?'

'Yeah.'

'You're drunk,' said Tom. 'I'm getting off.'

Tom left the bus and started walking through the streets. Elise stayed. She stayed on the bus for some time. Until the roads started to widen and the cobbled streets became intertwined with green stretches. The bus emptied of people, and soon she was the last passenger. She did not care and rarely took her gaze from the window. She waited patiently until she saw a small house at the end of a medium-sized path. Her attention was immediately taken. She looked on as the bus neared the path. The house was petite and seemingly unoccupied. She pressed the stop button and the bus stopped. She thanked the driver and got off the bus. She knew that the bus would soon return to town. She had stepped from the bus more in desperation than inspiration. The bus drove away, and Elise walked towards the path.

On the floor, at the beginning of the path she saw a small sign. *Darcy Lane*, it read. She stopped and looked around. The view was not exactly picturesque, but it was nice. She began walking along the path. As she neared the house, she looked out for any occupants. It seemed that she was alone. She reached the house and stopped in front of it.

The house was small, with white walls and a brown slate roof. The door was a bold red and the grass needed cutting. The curtains were drawn, and each window was firmly shut. She walked to the side of the house. At the back of the house, there was a small pond. The water was calm, with a carrier bag floating on the surface. She stood with folded arms. She turned and looked out across the fields.

'Darcy Lane,' she said to herself.

Chapter 4
Grace's Journal

Elise and Tom had been reading from Grace's journal for the past two hours. This was her first real effort to read from it. They read in Elise's bedroom. Outside, the day was miserable. Emmett had left for a day at the cricket club and the house felt empty without him. She felt obliged to pull the journal from under her bed. The journal was old and shabby. The pages were often ripped, and the front cover was stained by a splash of tea or coffee. On the inside cover, read a small note.

Hello Elise,
My name is Isabella Rathbone, but if you ever meet me, just call me Bell. I was friends with your mum, and she asked me to give you this journal if she could not. I might be wrong, but I think you may be 20 now. I thought this might be a good time to give it to you. I hope it finds you well. If you need to talk, I live at 14 Smithson St. Please feel free to visit.
Best Wishes
Bell x

So far, Elise had been disappointed by the journal. Many of the entries had been tarnished and those that were legible were mostly about men and friends. The entries were often short, more like briefs notes, rather than essays of expressed feelings. She started reading aloud but soon passed the journal to Tom.

'Please, can you read?' she asked. 'I'm finding it hard to read and listen.'

The journal started when Grace was still a teenager. It did not specify why the journal was started and truthfully, Elise did not care. In fact, she was unsure as to why she was reading from the journal at all.

Elise sat up and interrupted Tom as he spoke, 'Did I tell you that the people who burgled Grandad's shop got arrested?'

'No.'

'Well, they did. They've all been charged as well.'

'Emmett must be pleased.'

'Partly.'

'Partly?'

'He got a note under the shop door, telling him not to press charges.'

'Has he told the police?'

'Yeah. They say it's nothing to worry about.'

Tom continued to read, but Elise's attention waned. She sat back in bed and thought of Darcy Lane. Recently, she had thought of little else. The house had become fixed in her consciousness. She had visited it again, both in mind and reality. She had tried to think of other things. Her mother's journal, going back to school, remembering to take her medication, but nothing else seemed important. Elise rubbed her eyes.

'Are you listening?' asked Tom.

'Not really,' said Elise. She then stood and left the room. She returned a moment later with a small bottle of gin, two glasses and a bottle of tonic tucked under her arm.

'Do you want one?' she asked.

'Yeah, go on,' said Tom.

Elise made the drinks and passed a glass to Tom. 'So, are we giving up on the journal?' he asked.

'No,' said Elise. 'Can you please keep reading?'

Tom sat turning the pages in his hands. He drank and read with a steady tone. He read for a short while and then stopped. He closed the journal and placed it on his lap. 'I'm done for a while,' he said. 'I'm out of gin as well.'

'The gin's by the window,' said Elise. 'Help yourself.'

Tom stood and stretched. He walked towards the bottle and filled his glass. 'We should go out,' he said. 'Go do something, I'm sick of your house.'

'What is there to do?' she asked. 'Its cold outside.'

'We could go for a walk.'

'When do we ever go for a walk?'

'Anyway,' she continued. 'I'd like to carry on with the journal.'

'But you're not listening. I'm reading to the walls.'

'Please, let's carry on. I'll listen now.'

'All right, no problem,' he said. 'Just let me enjoy my gin for a second.'

He finished his gin and picked up the journal. He brought it back to the other side of the room and stood leaning against the window frame. He strolled through the pages with his hands. Elise pushed herself up against the wall and sat with her legs outstretched on the bed. She sat with the bottle of gin tucked between her legs. Tom continued through the pages until a smile appeared on his face. 'Entry 277,' he said. 'Elise is born.'

'Should I read it?' he continued.

'Yeah.'

'It's only a small one.'

'Read it.'

'Elise is born.'

He read through the words to himself. He was still surprised by the way Grace wrote. He could not form a solid picture of the woman in his mind. Each time that he thought he had understood her personality, the words changed, and the picture of Grace changed with them. Throughout the journal, there had been entries dedicated to many people. Often to Emmett, friends, and a cocktail of men. Tom was pleased to see that this entry was dedicated to Elise.

'Are you ready?' he asked.

Elise nodded.

He coughed and started to read.

'Elise is born
Entry 277

Elise was born yesterday. She's with my dad now. He's very excited. He loves the name too. I think he's surprised that I thought of it. The truth is that I'm unsure how to act. The birth was horrible. I couldn't wait for it to be over. It all seemed so sudden. The nurse at the hospital told me that Elise looks like me. I can't see it myself, but I hope it's true. I didn't drink during the whole pregnancy, and although that's normal for most people, I'm proud that I lasted the whole time. I had one cigarette but put it out straight away. It felt like it was hurting the baby and it just tasted bitter around my lips. Throughout the pregnancy, all I could think about was the things that could happen to my child. Now she's been born and I'm worried. I'm worried that Elise will be too much like me, that she grows up too scared to try things or even be happy. I chose the name Elise because I don't know anyone called Elise, and the truth is, I don't want her to be like anyone I know. I don't know. I just hope this is the start of something new for me.
Grace Rose'

Tom closed the journal and held it under his arm. He looked at Elise, who sat with the bottle of gin in her hands. 'That can't have been fun,' he said.

She smiled. 'It all sounds a bit stupid now, doesn't it?'

'Does it not bother you?'

'Of course it bothers me.'

She leant her head back against the wall. 'Thanks for reading it anyway,' she said.

She then stood and began walking around the room. She had blushed, clearly unsettled by her mother's words.

Tom threw the journal onto the bed. 'More gin,' he said.

Elise soon relaxed. She stood with Tom, drinking by the window. She looked out across the concrete. 'I found something the other day,' she said. 'Something good.'

'What was it?'

'A house.'

'A house?'

'Yeah, a nice little house.'

'When did you find this house?'

'Do you remember when we went to The Phonebox and I stayed on the bus?'

'Yeah, when you were drunk.'

'Well, I stayed on the bus for ages and found a house.'

'Where?'

'Darcy Lane. It's outside town.'

She described Darcy Lane to Tom. The walls, the roof and the pond sitting at the back of the house.

Tom grinned. 'Thinking of moving, are you?' he asked. 'I could imagine you living in the country.'

'It's not the country,' she said. 'It's just away from town.'

'Who lives there?' he asked.

She shrugged, 'I've never seen anyone there. I don't think anyone lives there.'

She continued to describe the house. She seemed to loosen as she spoke. 'There's a nice view,' she said. 'Space as well. There's space everywhere.'

'Darcy Lane,' he said. 'Very nice.'

'The grass needs cutting and the windows cleaning, but yeah, it is nice.'

'You seem set,' he said. 'You'll have to show me sometime.'

She brushed past him and took a coat from the wardrobe. She pulled the coat over her shoulders and grinned. 'I'll show you,' she said. 'I'll take you there.'

Tom sat on the bed. 'What, now?' he asked.

'I didn't mean now. Its cold outside, you said yourself.'

She pushed her hands grumpily into her coat pockets, 'You were the one that said we should go out.'

'Yes, but you said we were staying in. I've got used to the idea of staying in.'

Elise pulled Tom's jacket from the side and threw it towards him. 'Come on,' she said. 'I want to show it you.'

He sat up. 'Do you really want to go?'

'Yes,' she said, 'I really want to go!'

Tom started to put on his jacket. 'What about the journal?' he asked. 'Don't you want to read to the end?'

Elise smiled. 'I already know how it ends,' she said, and left the room.

Chapter 5
Bell's House

The morning was cold, but she smiled from under her jacket. She had awoken early, put gloves on her hands, socks on her feet and started walking towards Bell's House with Tom. She was pleased.

'I wonder if she'll recognise me?' she asked. 'Maybe I should've brought the journal.'

Elise's initial impression of Bell was vague. She could not remember her from her childhood. The journal showed Grace and Bell to be close friends from a young age. Grace was quiet and childish, while Bell was erratic and mischievous. The journal showed a new side to her mother's personality. The entries showed vigour, and even joy. She was pleased to read about her mother as a younger woman.

'She might not be in,' said Tom. 'You should've called her.'

'She didn't leave her number.'

'I thought you were done with the journal, anyway.'

'I am.'

'Then why are we here?'

'I need to speak to her about something.'

Elise pulled her jacket into her frame and continued through the streets. She scurried with hurried step.

'Slow down,' said Tom. 'You're going too fast.'

They crossed roads, turned corners, and soon arrived at Smithson Street.

'14, was it?' asked Tom. 'It shouldn't be too far away.'

Elise walked with shallow breath, 'I'm nervous,' she said. 'Why am I nervous?'

Tom grinned and walked slightly ahead. 'It's up here,' he said.

Smithson Street was wider than the streets she was used to, the houses seemed relaxed, as though they had enough room between themselves and their neighbours. The pavements were clean, children played at the top of the street and the cars seemed new and cared for.

Tom noted the number of each house as he passed. '8,' he said, '8, 10, 12, 14… 14 we're here.'

Elise opened the gate and walked towards the front door. 'Here we are,' she said, and knocked loudly.

Bell's house pleased Elise. It was semi-detached, red brick and had a small welcome mat outside the front door.

'I might get one of those,' she said, pointing towards the mat.

She stepped forwards and looked through the glass in the door. She saw a figure coming towards her and stepped back. The door opened and behind it stood a thin woman with a pair of slippers on her feet. The woman had a slight arch in her back, as though she had spent too much time looking at her feet.

'Elise?' she asked. 'Shit, you look like your mum.'

Bell reached out to hug Elise, who stood seemingly unsure, with her arms by her side.

'Hug her back then,' said Tom.

Elise wrapped her arms around Bell's thin frame. 'Sorry,' she said quickly.

'Come in,' said Bell. 'It's so good to see you.'

Elise followed Bell inside. 'I love your house,' she said. 'It's lovely.'

Bell turned, and smiled, 'Thanks. Some tea?'

'Yes!' replied Tom, as he stepped inside the house. 'Please.'

Tom closed the door and took off his shoes. 'Two sugars please,' he continued.

Elise followed Bell towards the kitchen. As they walked through the hallway, she saw pictures of a man and a small boy. She looked towards one of the frames, picked it up and put it back down quickly. 'Who are they?' she asked.

Bell smiled again. 'That's my husband and that's my son,' she said. 'You should meet them.'

'What are their names?' asked Elise.

'John and Junior. We called him after his dad.'

'That's a bit dodgy, isn't it?'

'I know. It was his idea.'

'They seem nice, anyway.'

'Thanks. This way.'

They reached the kitchen and Bell started to make tea. She filled the kettle, set out three cups and waited. She stood leaning against the kitchen side. 'Honestly,' she said. 'It's like standing right next to her. Your mum, I mean.'

Elise rested at the side of the kitchen. 'You're not the first person to say that,' she said. 'She was my mum, after all.'

The kitchen was brightened by natural light. There were magnets on the fridge, and outside, there was a small garden. Elise smiled at the sight.

Tom followed Elise into the kitchen and rested beside her.

'Two sugars, was it?' asked Bell.

'Please,' said Tom.

'Why'd you take your shoes off?' asked Bell.

Tom looked towards his feet, and said, 'Just a habit.'

Bell smiled and pointed towards the front room. 'Do you want to sit in the front room?' she asked.

'I'm fine here,' said Elise.

The kettle boiled, and Bell made the tea. She put sugar in one of the cups and passed it to Tom. She passed another cup to Elise and stood with her arms folded.

'I was expecting to see you sooner,' she said.

'I wasn't sure,' said Elise. 'About coming, but thanks for bringing me the journal.'

'You must've been surprised,' said Bell.

'Yeah, just a little.'

'I thought this was the right time.'

'So, my mum asked you to give me the journal?'

'Yeah, she always had this strange feeling that she wouldn't be around to see you grow up. It always used to annoy me when she said it.'

'She was right.'

'Yeah, I suppose she was,' said Bell.

'Anyway,' she continued. 'The boy here…sorry I forgot your name?'

'Tom.'

'Tom, said you were in hospital. Is everything okay?'

'Yeah, I'm fine.'

'She's as good as new,' said Tom.

Elise and Tom took a sip of tea. They still wore the cold on their faces.

'Are you sure you don't want to talk in the front room?' said Bell. 'It's much warmer in there.'

Elise took another sip and shook her head, 'It's fine,' she said. 'We're happy here.'

The room soon became silent, and Elise and Bell exchanged nervous glances. Bell seemed fidgety. Perhaps she felt guilty, or perhaps this was just her nature. She reminded Elise of her mother, or at least of what she could remember about her. She noticed similarities in the way they stood.

'So, you and my mum were good friends?' she asked. 'How'd you meet?'

Bell grinned. 'We were best friends,' she said. 'We met at school; we must've only been four or five.'

'We used to fall out all the time,' she continued.

'What did you fall out about?'

'I was very moody, and she was very impatient. She used to get sick of me and walk off. It was quite funny, looking back.'

Bell took a sip and let out a childish smile. 'So,' she said, 'I'm guessing you're here to talk about the journal?'

Elise straightened. 'No, actually,' she said, 'I'm here about something else.'

'What?'

'So, you and my mum were close?'

'Yeah.'

'Did you ever meet someone called Jack Clapham?'

Tom put down his cup. 'You came here to talk about him?' he asked. 'The guy from The Phonebox?'

Elise snarled. 'I didn't ask you,' she said. 'I asked Bell.'

Elise had been thinking about Jack lately. She had walked to Bell's house, intent on understanding the man who had offered to help her.

'I was introduced to him by a friend,' she continued. 'He said that he knew my mum.'

Bell's features seemed to narrow with the mention of Jack's name. The fragility of her face seemed to harden.

'Jack Clapham? Yeah, I know him. What did he say to you?' she asked.

Elise became nervous with Bell's sudden change in tone. 'He said that he could help me,' she mumbled. 'He told me to call him if I ever needed anything. He gave me his number.'

Bell started to fuss and fidget, 'He knew your mum, but they weren't close. He grew up across the street from her. I don't think I ever saw them speak.'

'I told you there was something off about him,' said Tom.

'When did he speak to you?' asked Bell.

'Not long ago. He saw me in a bar and came over.'

'And he said he could help you?'

'Yeah, he said to call him if I ever needed anything.'

'Help you with what?'

'I don't know. He didn't say.'

Elise took another sip of tea, 'I was surprised when I didn't see his name mentioned in the journal, not once.'

Bell's distaste was evident. 'You should stay away from him,' she said. 'Let me know if he ever tries to speak to you .again.'

Elise scratched the hair at the back of her head and placed her cup on the side. 'I will,' she said. 'I'll tell you.'

'So, that's all you wanted to talk about?' asked Bell. 'Just about that, nothing about the journal?'

'I've still not finished it,' she said 'It's long.'

'You should read it,' said Bell. 'It might help you understand her.'

Bell gestured towards the door at the back of the house. 'Let's talk out here,' she said. 'I need a cigarette.'

Outside, Bell and Elise sat on white plastic chairs. Tom stood, leaning against the wall behind them.

Elise looked out across the garden. 'How long have you lived here?' she asked.

Bell lit her cigarette. 'Five years now. It's great,' she said. 'It's what I've always wanted.'

Elise smiled. 'Yeah, I know the feeling,' she said.

Bell sat and started to smoke, 'Junior loves the garden,' she said. 'He's always out here.'

'Yeah, I can tell,' replied Elise. 'I can't imagine the footballs are yours.'

Bell grinned and pulled her cigarette. As she smoked, Elise saw scraps of Bell as a younger woman. The way she held the cigarette and the way her face fell when she thought that she was not being watched.

'You remind me of my mum,' she said.

'I do?' replied Bell. 'You're the one that looks just like her.'

'The way you act, I mean. She used to smoke like that.'

'I feel like I'm back in 1994, sat next to you,' said Bell.

'1994?'

'Yeah, when I was younger and prettier.'

Bell finished her cigarette and stood. 'Its cold out here,' she said. 'Let's go back inside.'

Elise looked over her shoulder towards Tom. 'We should go soon,' she said.

'No!' said Bell. 'You're staying. I'll tell you some stories about your mum, stories that she wouldn't have put in the journal!'

Chapter 6
Will You Stay?

It was late autumn. The night was quiet and Elise had been waiting outside the home of Jack Clapham for the past fifteen minutes. She sat with Tom.

'We should go,' he said. 'He's not seen us yet. We can go now and he'll never know.'

She glanced impatiently towards him. 'I told him that I'd meet him. He knows I'm coming,' she said. 'I told him that I'd be here at eight.'

'Why do you want to meet him? Are you tapped?' he asked. 'Do you not remember what Bell told you?'

'I regret letting you come now.'

'I'm just telling you the truth.'

'I didn't ask for the truth. I asked for a lift.'

'I offered, actually. You're welcome, by the way.'

Elise sat, anxiously playing with her hands. She had surrendered to temptation, having called, and told Jack that she wanted to meet. He was pleased.

'What took you so long?' he asked. 'Come to my house next week. I'll text you the address.'

'Why your house?' Elise asked.

'Privacy's better,' replied Jack. 'We can have a proper talk. I'll see you soon.'

Jack had been a fixture in her thoughts. She had thought about him as she walked, ate with her grandfather, and rested her head at night. She had called him in desperation, but as she waited outside his house, she was worried that she had made the wrong decision.

'Fuck this,' continued Tom. 'We should go.'

'I'm here now,' said Elise. 'I can't go home now.'

Jack's home sat between thin streets. Elise rarely ventured this far across town and the unfamiliarity had started to breed concern. Jack's house was grand.

'It's a big house,' said Tom. 'I wasn't expecting this. What does he do again?'

'He owns a garage.'

'It must be busy, to pay for all this.'

'Must be.'

'You look nervous,' said Tom, 'Are you scared?'

'No,' she replied. 'Not nervous at all.'

She sat with sweat in the palms of her hands. She had already tried to leave the car, but something had pulled her back. Instead, she sat and looked out at the house from across the street. She curled. Her face was tense, and she could not sit still. She had planned to make the journey alone. She had told her grandfather that she was going out with friends from school and he was pleased to see her leave. She left the house to see Tom rummaging through the bins.

'What are you doing?' she asked.

'My dad's lost his watch. He thinks he might have thrown it out by mistake. Where are you going at this time?'

'To meet some friends from school.'

'You don't have any friends from school.'

'I do.'

'Who?'

'Chloe and Lucy.'

'You can't stand them. Where are you really going?'

'To meet Jack Clapham at his house.'

'Fuck off.'

'Don't judge me, please.'

'Hold on, I'll take you.'

They drove through the streets together. As they drove, Tom remained stout in his apprehensions.

'Why are you doing this?' he asked. 'This is the start of something bad. I can tell.'

Elise ignored his warnings. In fact, she was silent for most of the journey. She nodded, murmured, and looked from the window. They drove until she sat up in her seat.

'The next right,' she said. 'Dreston Road, number 26.'

They arrived at the house and Tom parked across the road. They waited there until she became impatient.

'What time is it?' she asked.

'Seven-forty-five,' replied Tom.

She opened the car door hurriedly. 'I'm going,' she said. 'I've had enough of waiting.'

'Should I come with you?'

'What, my knight in shining armour, are you?'

'Piss off.'

'I'd rather go alone,' she said.

'Should I stay outside?'

'No,' she repeated. 'I'll find my own way home, but thanks. I'll see you soon.'

She opened the car door and stepped out onto the street. The cold was noticeable, and she shivered slightly. She crossed the street and stood outside number 26. She knocked and waited. Inside, she heard voices and the sounds of footsteps. She turned and looked back towards Tom. He seemed further away than she expected. She heard someone walking along the hallway and stepped back. The front door opened, and she was happy to see a familiar face. It was Elijah.

'Elise,' he said. 'Welcome, welcome.'

She smiled and stepped inside. 'Who's here?' she asked.

'Me, Jack and Frankie,' he replied. 'They're in there, the room at the end of the hallway.'

Jack's home was beautiful. Pictures hung, and the hallway was laid with a handsome wood. Elijah closed the front door behind her and followed her along the hallway. She could hear laughing as she approached the door.

'Come in!' said a voice. 'Come in!' it repeated.

She walked into the room to see Jack and Frankie smoking from the corners of their mouths.

Jack stood and greeted her. 'Aha!' he said. 'She arrives. I thought you were ignoring us!'

Elise smiled and looked towards Frankie. He sat with his face, unmoving. He reached out a stray hand and embraced her loosely.

'Evening,' he said. 'There's a seat for you over there.'

Elise walked further into the room and her attention was taken by a large picture hanging on the wall. The picture showed a man and a woman, sat together, eating grapes.

'Nice picture,' she said.

'So, you noticed it?' asked Jack. 'This is my prized possession. Pretty isn't it?'

She walked towards the picture and looked at it carefully. 'I didn't think you were the sort of person to collect art,' she said.

Jack smiled, 'Na, just this.'

She took off her coat and sat down.

'Get her a drink,' said Jack.

Elijah left and disappeared to the kitchen. He returned with a small glass of gin and a blushed face.

'Gin,' he said, as he passed her the glass.

She looked at Jack. 'How'd you know I like gin?'

'At The Phonebox,' said Jack. 'I see everything. It's a gift.'

'Thanks,' said Elise.

Elijah nodded. His once youthful expression had become stern, as though he had become aware of his own demeanour. He picked up his own glass and sat down next to Frankie on the settee. Elise sat and looked around the room. Much like the hallway, the front room was pleasing. It had regular things: a television, plants, and a selection of books on shelves and windowsills. It even had pictures of Jack as a younger man, with friends, and perhaps family.

She took a sip and looked towards him. 'What did you mean when you said you could help me?' she asked.

'Straight away? You don't waste time.'

'I was just wondering.'

'Well, I own a garage. You could work there, that's help.'

'At the garage? I'm not the car type.'

'Doing the books, on the phones, just helping out.'

'I don't know how to do the books.'

'I can teach you. Did you pass maths at school?'

'Yeah, I did well in maths.'

'Perfect,' said Jack. 'There you go. You've been here two minutes and you already have a job. You can start on Monday.'

'I work at my grandad's shop on Mondays.'

'Tuesday, then. you can start on Tuesday.'

He stood and took a bottle of rum from the side. 'I'm glad you're here,' he said. 'I wasn't sure if you were going to call.'

Elise watched Jack as he moved. He was someone who commanded attention. His walk was loose, and his face was peculiar. He sat back down and picked up his glass from the floor. He poured the rum and started to ask her about herself.

'So, are you enjoying the freedom?'

'I do miss the unit sometimes. I had a friend. She was very funny.'

'Where were you again?' asked Frankie.

'The psychiatric unit.'

'What were you doing there?'

'Answering questions,' she said. 'Just answering a lot of questions, really.'

Frankie grinned. 'Better now, though?' he asked.

Elise took a brief sip. 'Perfect,' she said.

'How do you two know each other?' she continued.

'Me and Frankie have been friends since we were teenagers. I'm helping him get back on his feet. He's just been released from prison. Isn't that right, Frankie?'

'When did you get out?' asked Elise.

'18 months ago,' said Frankie. 'Feels like yesterday.'

Frankie started to tell stories about his time in prison. Elise listened sparingly. He told a story about a fight he had with a fellow inmate over a game of pool. Elise smiled and laughed where necessary. They continued to drink together. Elise and Elijah remembered old stories from the estate while Jack smoked cigarettes at the back of the house. Elise's nerves soon settled. She was comfortable with Jack from the start. Much like Dr Laghari at the psychiatric unit, he had a way of making her feel comfortable. He asked her questions about herself and listened intently. He seemed sincere, vulnerable even.

'So, how'd you know my mum?' she asked. 'You lived across the street, didn't you?'

'Yeah, she lived across the street from me.'

'What was she like?'

'She was beautiful, man. Saved me from getting a beating once, too.'

'My mum saved you?'

'Yeah, from my brothers. They were always going for me. I was the youngest by a few years. One day after school, somewhere in the winter months, they were giving me a proper kicking outside our house. Your mum was watching from her bedroom window. She came outside and told them to leave me alone.'

'And did they?'

'Yeah, they did. I think they were scared of her. She was always hanging around with the older boys at school.'

'Wow.'

'It must have been a few weeks before they went for me again. The easiest few weeks of my life.'

'I didn't know she was like that.'

'What?'

'I don't know…authoritative.'

'Yeah well, you only saw the worst of her. That's not how I remember her.'

The night soon passed. Elijah drank and fell asleep on the settee while Frankie drove home. Elise and Jack continued to drink. As they both became drunken, they started to speak more freely. She told him about the burglary at her grandfather's store. She leant her head back against the chair and looked towards the ceiling.

'He's been on edge for the past month,' she said. 'After it all happened. He's not been sleeping.'

Jack sat with one leg crossed over the other. 'What did the police say?' he asked.

'They've arrested the people who did it, but Grandad's worried. They're trying to stop him pressing charges.'

'Who?' he asked.

She leant forwards and rested her glass on the floor. 'Someone put a note under the door of the shop, telling him not to press charges. Threats, really.'

Jack told Elise that *things would work themselves out*, and she believed him. As he spoke, Jack's tone had quietened, his bravado had relaxed, and Elise was encouraged by his true nature.

She stood and returned to the picture on the wall. 'Why a man and a woman?' she asked.

Jack stood and walked towards her. 'Why anything?' he said. 'I once fell in love with a woman by the way she put on her coat. Really, what else is there?'

Jack told Elise that he had found the picture on the street. 'Someone had thrown it out,' he said. 'I couldn't believe it.'

He told her that he took the picture home, cleaned it, and hung it on his wall. 'It's been hanging there, ever since,' he said.

Elise smiled. 'I found something after I met you,' she said.

'After The Phonebox?' replied Jack.

'Yeah,' she said. 'The fields in this picture. It reminds me of it.'

'What did you find?'

'A house.'

'A house?'

'Yeah, strange, I know.'

'Where?'

'Darcy Lane.'

She began to describe Darcy Lane. She described the walls, the roof, the door, and the small crack at the top of the house. She described the grass, the pond, and the windows.

She told Jack how she found the house. 'I was on the bus,' she said. 'It was like it took me straight to it.'

Jack seemed pleased. 'It sounds really nice,' he said. 'We should go sometime.'

Elise turned. 'When you said you could help me,' she said. 'You didn't mean at the garage. You meant something else, I could tell.'

'Yeah.'

'There's something you're not telling me.'

'If I tell you, you'll leave.'

'I won't.'

'You will.'

'Well, tell me and find out.'

He stepped back and took a sip from his glass. 'It's too early,' he said. 'We've just met.'

Elise raised her tone. 'If you don't tell me, I'll leave,' she said.

Jack laughed, 'I've had too many drinks to be talking about this. Maybe we should call it a night. I can get you a taxi.'

She nudged towards him. 'There has to be something else,' she said. 'How else could you afford this place? Business that good, is it? Just tell me. I should know who I'm talking to.'

'Okay,' he said. 'You're right. You should know who you're talking to.'

He stretched out his hands. 'So, you want to know how I afforded this place?' he asked. 'Well, we rob. Frankie did seven years inside, but I've always been lucky.'

Jack ran his hand through his hair. It was short and brown. 'We're just like the people who burgled your grandad's store,' he said. 'So, leave if you want to. We don't do it often, only if it's a sure thing.'

'So, you're burglars?' asked Elise.

Jack smiled, 'No, I'm a mechanic.'

She walked past Jack and sat on the settee next to Elijah. 'I was told to stay away from you,' she said. 'People have warned me about you.'

Jack sat down in the chair opposite her and began playing with his sleeve. 'Well, that didn't take long,' he said.

'So,' he continued. 'Now that you know about me, will you stay?'

Chapter 7
Darcy Lane

Elise and Tom had been sat looking at Darcy Lane for the last hour. She sat peacefully. She sat on the fence facing the house, smiling with her eyes.

Tom sat less peacefully. 'It's too cold,' he said. 'We should've stayed at The Phonebox.'

Tom had hoped to stay away from Darcy Lane. He was happy inside, hidden in the corner of the bar. But Elise insisted they made the trip.

'I haven't been all week,' she said. 'What if something's changed?'

Tom snarled. 'It's a house,' he said. 'What could've changed?'

However, he eventually buckled to her demands. He finished his drink, stood, and tucked his chair under the table.

'We're only going for half an hour,' he said. 'I'm not staying all afternoon, like last time.'

The pair left the bar together. They walked out into the cold and took the bus towards Darcy Lane. As they stepped onto the bus, the bus driver smiled towards them. They had taken the journey so many times that the driver had started to recognise them.

'Back again?' he asked. 'Should I guess where you two are going?'

'Two tickets to Darcy Lane, please.'

'Two tickets to Darcy Lane, there you go.'

Elise took her tickets and sat at the back of the bus with a half-smile on her face. Tom merely sulked and chewed on his nails. They stayed on the bus and soon they were the last passengers.

'We might be the only people who know about this place,' she said. 'And the bus driver.'

'Lucky us.'

'Are you not happy?'

'No, I was happy at The Phonebox.'

They reached Darcy Lane and she thanked the bus driver.

'I'll be back in an hour to pick you up,' he joked.

They left the bus and began walking along the path. As she walked, Elise opened her arms in celebration. She took a quick look around the house and took her place on the fence.

'This is the best view,' she said. 'You can see the whole house from here.'

She clasped her hands around the wood and let her feet dangle from the ground. As she looked out, so cheerfully, Tom could not fathom her fascination. He slumbered to the fence and wiped his nose.

'Back,' he said. 'Back for another day, looking at an empty house.'

She ignored his moans and continued to look cheerfully from the fence. She started to daydream, imagining early mornings in the summertime and afternoons in the autumn.

'Have you told Emmett about this place?' asked Tom.

'No.'

'Are you going to?'

'Why, should I?'

'If it's so important, maybe he should know.'

'I didn't say it was so important. I just like it here.'

'You should tell him.'

'You should stop.'

She started to tell Tom about the changes she would make to the house if she could. Firstly, she would paint the front room in fresh paint. The curtains were closed so she could not see inside, but she presumed that the walls would need to be painted. Then she would buy a selection of plants, new furniture and cushions to match the settee.

'Grandad could help me with all that,' she said. 'He has a good eye for that sort of thing.'

Next, she would buy a rug for the centre of the room and a glass table to hold it in place. She would buy new curtains.

'I don't like brown,' she said. 'Those curtains would have to go.'

She would then put pictures of herself and her grandfather around the room and buy a comfortable chair, where he could sit and read.

'He loves to read,' she said. 'He'd sit there all day if he could.'

She would clean the front room each day. 'The front room's the most important room in the house,' she said. 'It's the room people see first.'

She would spend time in the garden. 'We would have to buy some chairs,' she said. 'I don't think they'd be too expensive.'

She would swim in the pond and dry off at the back of the house. She would cut the grass every fortnight.

'It annoys me how long it is,' she said. 'That might be the first thing I do, actually, cut the grass.'

Elise turned and pointed towards the path. 'I would clear the path of all the stones,' she said. 'I think that would make a big difference.'

She titled her head towards the house. 'That would be a good start,' she said. 'I'd leave the front door the same colour too. It has definitely grown on me.'

'What do you think?' she continued.

'Yeah, it's a pretty colour.'

'What about the rest of it?'

'Yeah, it sounds all right. Not sure about swimming in that pond, though.'

'And then there's the bedrooms, of course. I've not really thought about the bedrooms yet.'

'No rush.'

'I'll think about them tonight. Maybe blue for the walls. Something unimposing.'

Tom grimaced but smiled as she looked towards him. 'It all sounds great,' he said.

She returned the smile. 'Don't look so nervous,' she said. 'It's just an idea.'

As the afternoon passed, Tom began to wriggle on the fence.

He sighed. 'We should go home. I'm sick of this place,' he said. 'We've been here for fucking ages, now. It looks like it might rain as well. I don't want to get wet. I've just washed these clothes.'

Elise looked towards the sky. Her eyes were wide and bright. 'It's not going to rain,' she said. 'And what are we going to do at home? What's so special about home?'

'Have some tea, relax, not be outside.'

'It's because you're not talking. You're bored because you're not talking.' Elise was lively. 'Ask me something?' she said. 'Anything.'

Tom brushed at his pants with his hands, 'Really? Anything?'

'Anything, mate.'

'And you have to tell me?'

'Uh huh.'

'There is one thing I want to know.'

'Ask me.'

'Why were you sent away? To the psychiatric unit, I mean. Your grandad wouldn't tell anyone.'

Her face tightened. 'Why'd you want to know that?' she asked.

'You said anything,' he replied. 'That's my question. That's what I want to know.'

She turned away from him. She had turned a shade of crimson. 'I'm not telling you that,' she said. 'Ask me something else, you nosy bastard.'

He shrugged, 'You said you'd tell me. Anything, you said.'

'I didn't think you'd ask that.'

'Just tell me stop being weird.'

'I've spent enough time talking about it. Two years, actually.'

'Don't tell me, then. Do you think I'll laugh or something?'

'You better not fucking laugh.'

'You don't have to tell me if you don't want to. I just thought I'd ask.'

'Okay,' she continued. 'If you really want to know, I'll tell you. I was in sixth form, that's where it started.'

'School?'

'Yeah, school.'

'Okay, so you're at school.'

Elise exhaled sharply. Her head was lowered, and she was looking at her feet, 'So, I was at school, in the library and one of the teachers tapped me on the shoulder and told me that my grandad was waiting for me in reception.'

'Okay, nothing traumatic so far.'

'So, I go to reception and see my grandad waiting for me. I knew that there was something wrong straight away. He looked scared. I left school with him and my grandad drove me home. I thought he was going to take me to the shop. He'd do that sometimes – take me out of sixth form if the shop was busy or he needed help. He wouldn't do it often, but sometimes, but this time he took me straight home. When we arrived home, there was a police car waiting outside our house.'

'Yeah.'

'When he saw us, the police officer, he got out of his car and followed me and Grandad inside. Grandad was still acting strange. He told me to sit down and gave me a glass of water. The police officer sat down and told me that the man who had killed my mum had committed suicide in prison. I was only seventeen at the time and I hadn't thought of him in ages. Of course, I'd thought of him, but not for long. Anytime I thought of him, I would try to distract myself or push the thoughts away somehow. It didn't always work but I would try. The police officer told me that many of the officers at the station still remembered the case and that they thought I should know about the man's death. The police officer stayed for a while after that. I think Grandad made him tea or something. The officer told me that there was help if I needed it and that the news would probably take a while to sink in. The officer almost seemed happy. It seemed like he expected me to be happy too. He spoke to me some more, but all I could think about was the man. It sounds strange, but I felt like I was back in the room with him. The police officer left after that and I asked Grandad if I could go back to school. He wouldn't let me and took me to get some ice cream.'

'So, the man killed himself?'

'He did.'

'What happened after the ice cream?'

'That's where things went wrong.'

'That doesn't sound good.'

'In the months after the news, things just started to change. I couldn't sleep. I'd never had problems sleeping, but I was up all night, every night. And if I did manage to fall asleep, I was having nightmares again. I hadn't had one in years, not since I was a kid, anyway. It's hard to describe but I could feel myself changing. I stopped speaking to my friends. I was too worried about how I'd act around them. I was hearing things that weren't there too – randomly throughout the day. I just started to feel really distant, detached almost.'

Elise's head was still leaning towards the ground. She folded her arms and tensed her body, 'They told me later at the unit that I was suffering from a form of psychosis. Something about childhood trauma being a factor. I can't remember the exact words they used. I don't think they were ever really sure what was wrong with me, but that's what they said. They kept using the word trigger. That's what they'd say. Trigger. Trigger. The news of the man's suicide was a trigger.'

'What, then you got taken away?'

'Not yet. Things got a bit worse first.'

'How?'

'I still wasn't sleeping. I don't think I'd had a proper night's sleep in maybe three months.'

'Okay.'

'I don't want to tell you the next bit.'

'You don't have to if you don't want to.'

'I started hallucinating. Apparently, it can be a part of psychosis, whatever was wrong with me. It's going to sound strange, but I started seeing my mum. It all started one afternoon. I was walking through town and I saw her getting on the bus, a little further along the street. I chased her, but she didn't see me and the bus drove away before I could stop it.'

'You saw your mum?'

'You don't have to believe me.'

'She died years back.'

'I know. I was hallucinating – badly.'

Elise lifted her head and looked towards him. Her eyes had dampened slightly. 'About a month after I saw her getting on the bus, I saw her again, eating breakfast in the cafe near the train station. So, I went inside and spoke to her. She told me that after she was attacked all those years ago, she'd left town. She said she left because she didn't want to cause me any more trouble. She told me that although she'd been injured, she didn't die that night. She said that she'd agreed to let my grandad look after me, and that as part of the agreement, she'd leave town and let me grow up in peace. She told me that after all these years, she'd decided to come back to town. She hugged me, asked for my address, and told me that she'd be in touch. She also told me not to tell my grandad about our conversation, as he would try and keep us apart. She then left the cafe. I remember, all the staff in the cafe were looking at me. I didn't understand why at the time, but it all makes sense now.'

'Elise.'

'Hold on. I may as well tell you the full story.'

'Over the next four or five months, I looked for my mum everywhere. I visited all the homeless communities, all the shelters and hostels I could find. I found an old picture of her in my grandad's room. I took it with me and showed it to everyone. I really thought I'd lost her until I saw her one morning from my bedroom window. She was walking through the alleys at the back of my house. I left my room and chased her. I caught up to her a few streets away. She was so happy to see me. She told me that she couldn't find my address and that she'd been looking for me the whole time. She said that she was leaving town and that I should come with her. She told me that she was leaving tomorrow and that if I wanted to come, I should meet her at 10 am by the bus stop outside the toy store in the town centre. I'd been looking for my mum for months, so I wasn't going to let her leave without me. That night, I packed my bags. I hid them under my bed, collected all the money I had and waited till the next morning. I waited till my grandad left for work and then I left too. I went early, I caught the bus into town and was outside the toy store for 9 am. I waited for nearly three hours, but she didn't come. I almost gave up and went home. But then I saw her, behind me, going into the toy store. She must've been looking for me, I thought. I took my bags and looked around the store, but I couldn't find her. Then I started to get angry. I started shouting and pushing toys from the shelves. A member of staff came over and tried to calm me down, but I hit her in the face. I started pushing over stands and two other members of staff pushed me from the store. I tried to get back in, but they wouldn't let me. A random woman then came behind me and tried to calm me down. I hit her too. The police were called, and I was taken away. At the station, I told them the story about my mum, the bus, the cafe, and the toy store. They kept me at the station and called my grandad. Then they took me to the unit for the first time.'

'You smashed up a toy store?'

'I was looking for my mum.'

'Why didn't you tell me all this?'

'Listen to it. Where would I even start?'

Tom puffed his cheeks. 'You're better now, though?' he asked.

Elise grimaced, 'Yeah I'm better. That's why they let me out.'

'I shouldn't have given you the journal.'

'I'm glad you gave it to me.'

'You don't still think she's alive, do you?'

'I never did. I was hallucinating. The medication stops all that.'

'Man, I feel bad.'

'Don't. I don't need pity.'

'I'm sorry. I just wasn't expecting all that.'

'How could you.'

She watched for Tom's reaction. He seemed uncomfortable.

'Do you think I'm crazy?' she asked.

'A little,' he said, smiling. 'That's some story.'

Tom's demeanour had changed instantly. It was as though he had become careful about his words and actions. He asked her questions about the unit and she answered briefly.

'I should have visited,' he said.

'Yeah, maybe.'

'Emmett didn't tell us anything.'

'I know. He felt guilty. He thought it was his fault. It wasn't, obviously.'

'Did he tell you that? That he thought it was his fault?'

'I could tell. He's not very good at hiding his feelings.'

She stepped from the fence. 'It's over now,' she said. 'It's time to move on.'

Tom continued to ask questions about the unit and she soon became tired of his enthusiasm.

'I've not annoyed you, have I?' he asked. 'By asking you about all this?'

Elise shook her head, 'I wouldn't have told you if I didn't want to. You would have found out at some point, anyway. It's hard to keep those sorts of things a secret.'

He stepped from the fence. 'Don't worry,' he said. 'I won't tell anyone.'

Elise became silent. She looked towards her feet and then up towards the sky. The day was overcast and rain threatened. As she glanced upwards, she held out a hand and drew the shape of the sun with her finger. She filled it in with her thumb and waited to feel the warmth of her skin.

'Thanks,' she said.

Chapter 8
Ordinary Man

One Month Later

'This was a good idea,' said Tom. 'We should come here more often.'

'What, the park?' replied Elise, rearranging herself on the bench. 'We should come to the park more often?'

'Look at all this green grass,' he continued. 'It's beautiful, actually.'

The park was almost empty. Stray pedestrians walked along the paths and the sun threatened through the clouds. The day was cold but enjoyable. Concrete intertwined with grass. Elise and Tom had not seen each other in some time, with the last months being difficult for their friendship. Elise had been spending much of her time at the garage with Jack, Frankie, and Elijah. She had become comfortable around them, even Frankie, who had begun to warm to her and include her in conversations. She helped with the books and made tea. Jack even offered to show her around an engine, but she refused. Because of her days at the garage, Tom and Elise had been seeing less of each other. She was partly pleased about this, since she had told him about the events that had led to her stay at the psychiatric unit, she felt that Tom had started to look at her differently. Perhaps she was just being paranoid. Elise had been thinking lately about her stay at the unit. She often woke up during the night, still thinking that she was a patient. Each time, it took her a few moments to realise that she was actually back home. Each time she was relieved.

She had been trying not to think of her stay at the unit. Although it was beneficial, and she was happy there, she was still embarrassed. She was twenty years old and there were still parts of her reality that she could not face. She struggled on the bench, pulled a flask from her pocket, and took a sip of gin.

'Why're you doing that?' asked Tom.

'What?'

'Drinking, in the morning. In a park.'

'Why not?'

'Think about it.'

'Jack got me the flask.'

'Yeah, you seem quite close now. It's strange how things change.'

Tom often asked her these questions, 'Why're you doing that? Why're you meeting with Jack Clapham?' he would ask. 'Why do you keep going to Darcy Lane? Why're you spending so much time at the garage?'

The more questions he asked, the more frustrated she would become. 'Just stop,' she would say. 'Just stop with all the questions.'

She took another sip of gin and put the flask in her pocket. She glanced towards him, and grinned. 'It's good to see you anyway,' she said. 'You've been hiding from me, haven't you?'

He returned the grin and leant back on the bench. 'I don't think I'd get along with your new friends,' he said. 'Anyway, I've been busy with work. My dad's been given a new contract. We've been working flat out for the past month.'

She looked out across the park. The sprouts of grass and trees reminded her of summertime at the unit. She had spent her last two summers at the unit, and despite her current concerns, there was parts of her stay that she remembered fondly. She sat and became nostalgic about her own madness. She thought about Dora and their days together. Dora had a way of making her laugh. Most people at the unit found her intimidating, but Elise always enjoyed their time together. Despite the affection Elise felt for Dora, it was Dora's story that had been plaguing her. Dora had been a patient at the unit for the last twelve years. She had been released once before but returned shortly after. Elise did not want to return to the unit, she wanted to stay a part of the outside world. She coughed and leant forwards on the bench. She rubbed her hands together and blew into them.

'I said I'd meet Jack soon,' she said. 'It's ten to eleven. I said I'd meet him at eleven.'

'You never mentioned it.'

'I knew you'd argue with me.'

'I wouldn't argue. I never argue. It's up to you if you meet him.'

'I said I'd meet him at the car park on the other side.'

'We should go then,' said Tom. 'It'll probably take us about ten minutes to get there.'

Tom waited till Elise stood and stood with her. She began walking at a pace.

'Excited to see him, are you?' he asked.

'Slow down,' he said. 'Ten minutes is plenty of time.'

They began walking together. They walked from the bench and along the path. The path was flanked by trees and covered with twigs and small stones. She took her flask from her pocket and took another sip. She held the flask towards Tom, but he shook his head.

'No thanks,' he said. 'I prefer mine in a glass.'

They continued along the path and passed a small playground. There was a group of children hiding under one of the slides.

'Get out from under there!' said an erratic woman. 'Go play!'

The children scattered and began playing on the swings and climbing frames. Elise smiled and remembered her days on the estate.

'Which car park?' asked Tom.

'The one over there.'

'Is he here yet?'

'He will be. He's always early. I could ask him to give you a lift home.'

'No, thanks. I told my mum I'd get her a few things from the shop.'

They walked until the path started to narrow. They could soon see a row of cars from behind a small gate.

'It's just that one,' she said. 'Are you sure you don't want a lift?'

Tom embraced her loosely and began walking away. 'Another time,' he said. 'I'll walk today.'

'See you soon!' she said.

Tom turned. 'See you soon!' he repeated.

She continued along the path and through the gate. As she walked onto the car park, she saw a silver BMW parked in the corner. She walked towards the car and Jack waved from over the steering wheel. She skipped across the car park and got inside.

'You look cold,' he said. 'Your cheeks are red.'

'It's England, it's always cold,' she replied.

'So, where are we going?' she continued.

'I want to take you somewhere,' said Jack.

'Okay.'

'But I don't know where it is.'

'I don't understand.'

'You're going to have to tell me. I want to go to Darcy Lane.'

'Why?'

'You're always talking about it. I want to see it.'

Jack pulled the seat belt across his frame. He lowered the window on his side of the car and started to smoke. He pulled the cigarette from his lips. 'So, yes?' he said. 'We can go?'

Elise shrugged. 'Yeah, we can go. Pull out of here and go left.'

Jack pulled away from the car park and onto the main road. He asked Elise to direct him and she did. As he drove, he flicked on the radio with his finger and music started to play quietly.

'Who's at the garage?' she asked.

'Frankie. There isn't much to do. I told him I'd be back soon.'

'Did the Fiat get sorted?'

'Yeah, Elijah took care of it. We'd be lost without him, wouldn't we?'

'You would, maybe.'

'Are you still enjoying it? At the garage?'

'Yeah,' said Elise. 'I like it.'

Jack followed the roads from town. They drove between the streets and fallen leaves.

'Why'd you want to see it?' she asked. 'Darcy Lane?'

Jack laughed, 'You talk about it enough. I want to see what all the fuss is about. And anyway, there's something I need to ask you.'

She pulled the flask from her pocket and took a sip, 'What do you want to ask me? That sounds a bit ominous.'

He took the flask and took a short sip. 'Just wait,' he said. 'How far away are we?' he continued.

'About five minutes.'

'Well, you can wait five minutes.'

'You're not going to ask me to marry you, are you?'

'No, I hadn't planned to.'

'Good, because I hate weddings.'

'Why don't you like them? I love them.'

'They're all right, I suppose. Next right.'

He took the next right and opened the car up along the road.

'This is out the way,' he said. 'How'd you even find it?'

'The bus,' said Elise. 'I told you.'

They drove a little further until she could see Darcy Lane approaching in the distance.

'There it is,' she said. 'Turn left along that path – the one coming up.'

He turned and drove along the path. He scowled as he heard the stones clattering against his car. 'Rural,' he said.

They drove and parked outside the house. Elise loosened her seatbelt and stretched out her arms. 'This is it,' she said. 'This is the place.'

Jack stepped from the car and walked towards the house. He stood with his hands on his hips. She followed him.

'What do you think?' she asked.

Jack turned. 'It looks like a house,' he said.

He walked towards the front door and knocked several times. 'Who lives here?' he asked.

'No one,' she replied. 'I've never seen anyone here.'

Jack pulled another cigarette from his pocket and lit it. He walked to the side of the house and looked out towards the garden.

'Nice little pond at the back,' he said.

She grinned, 'So, you like it?'

Jack flicked ash onto the floor. 'All that matters is that you like it,' he said. 'But yeah, I do like it.'

'The grass could do with a cut though,' he said.

'I know,' said Elise, scratching the side of her head. 'It's only getting longer as well.'

Jack walked away from the house and sat on the bonnet of his car. 'Sit with me,' he said.

She walked and leant on the bonnet next to him.

'So, you want this place?' he asked.

Elise shrugged. 'I just like it here,' she said.

Jack seemed to grit his teeth. 'I brought you here for a reason,' he said. 'A few months ago, you asked me what I did, how I afforded my house.'

'Yeah, I remember.'

'But I didn't tell you why I do it.'

'All right.'

'I do it for this,' said Jack, pointing towards Darcy Lane. 'Because if there's something you want, you must take it.'

He stood up from the car and took a quick drag of his cigarette. 'That's why I brought you here,' he said. 'So you don't forget.'

'We have a job coming up,' he continued.

'A job?'

'Yeah, something to get you started. If you want to, of course.'

'A burglary, you mean?'

'Yeah. Don't worry. It's a sure thing. Something easy to get you started.'

'Where is it? The job?'

'We can talk about the details later,' he said, as he wiped a piece of ash from his jacket. 'All that matters now is that you want to do it. For this place, for yourself.'

'I'd prefer to know the details before I agree to anything,' she said.

'I thought this is what you wanted?'

'it is.'

'I can't tell you the details yet. I need to speak to Frankie. He doesn't know I'm telling you this.'

'Does he not want me involved?'

'I don't know. That's what I need to speak to him about.'

'Why would he not want me involved?'

'He gets very nervous after his last sentence. He tries to hide it, but he does.'

Elise sat with Jack, and once again told her plans for Darcy Lane to anyone who would listen. He revelled in her excitement. He asked questions, smoked cigarettes, and took short sips of gin from her flask.

'So,' he said, 'about the job. Are you interested?'

She took a short sip and nervously diverted his persistent stare.

'I want to know the details first,' she said. 'It's important.'

'Well, I can't tell you the details yet,' he replied. 'But I'll speak to Frankie soon, I promise.' He reassured her with a gentle nudge on the arm. He then started to tell stories and jokes.

Elise laughed. Her face ran with pleasure. They stayed for a while longer until Jack's phone started to ring for the second time in as many minutes.

'That'll be Frankie,' he said. 'I'll take you home. I have to get back to the shop. I told him I'd only be half an hour.'

'Can't we stay for a little longer?' she asked.

'I've already been too long. We can come back another time.'

'When?'

'Whenever you like, but come on, we have to go. You know how moody he gets.'

65

They got back into the car and she seemed to retreat slightly.

'Don't look so upset,' he said. 'We can come back.'

Jack started the engine. 'I like this place,' he said, 'but the stones are a nightmare.'

Elise smiled, 'I'm going to clear all the stones,' she said. 'And make it nice for cars.'

Jack curled the car around. 'Good,' he said. 'Maybe I'll visit more often then.'

He drove away from the house and along the road. She watched from the window as the house disappeared from view. They drove and Jack was jovial.

'You don't need to work on Friday,' he said. 'Elijah's coming in now.'

Elise sat with her hands tucked into her pockets. 'I'll still come,' she said. 'If you don't mind?'

Jack smiled. 'No,' he said. 'Of course I don't mind.'

They drove until the streets became familiar. Jack rubbed at his chin.

'Can I get to Hirst Street this way?' he asked.

Elise looked up. 'Yeah,' she said. 'Turn left at that shop up there.'

As they reached Hirst Street, Elise beamed and undid her seatbelt.

'Thanks for taking me to Darcy Lane,' she said.

'Don't worry about it. Think about what I said, okay?' said Jack, as he parked across the road from Number 44.

She opened the car door. 'See you,' she said.

He smiled. 'Yeah, enjoy your day,' he replied.

Elise crossed the road and walked into Number 44. Jack waited until she closed the door behind her and then looked up. Stood at his bedroom window was Emmett. The two of them held stare for a moment. Jack curled a half-smile and then pulled away from the kerb. Emmett's face remained stern. He watched as Jack drove away between the streets. He jabbed at the window with a closed fist. He then left his room and began walking down the stairs. As he walked, he whispered to himself, 'You can't let it happen again.'

Chapter 9
Elise

It was late. Doors had been locked, pavements swept of people and Elise was still not home. Emmett was worried. He peered through the curtains in the front room and waited by his bedroom window. He even took to the nearby streets in frantic search. Elise was twenty years old. She was independent and capable of original thought. Emmett trusted her. He gave her space, but she had not called, and she always would. Emmett had become panicked. He could not sit still. Perhaps she was with the man in the silver BMW. He returned to the streets briefly and then sat drinking tea at his kitchen table. He finished his tea and pushed away the cup. He walked from his house and knocked on the door of 43 Hirst Street.

'Tom, Tom!' he shouted.

'Tom, answer the door. It's Emmett!'

The door to 43 Hirst Street opened and behind it stood Tom, scratching the skin around his ear. 'Mr. Rose,' he said. 'It's a bit of a strange time for a visit.'

Emmett stepped forwards and peered into the house. 'Is Elise here?' he asked.

Tom gestured to speak, but he was interrupted by a shout from upstairs: 'Tom, who is it? Tell them to go away!'

Tom nudged to the foot of the stairs. 'Go back to bed, Mum,' he said. 'It's just Mr. Rose from next door. He's looking for Elise.'

He made a waving gesture towards his mum. 'Go back to bed,' he said. 'Get some rest.'

He returned to the door with a slightly reddened face. 'She's not here,' he said. 'I've not seen her.'

'So, you don't know where she is?' asked Emmett. 'You have no idea?'

Tom stepped out onto the street and pulled the door partly closed behind him. 'Why are you so worried?' he asked. 'She's probably just busy.'

Emmett turned and pointed across the road. 'I saw her with a man.' he said. 'He was driving a BMW. Is she with him?'

'I don't know. It's nothing to do with me.'

'So, you know him?'

'Yeah I know him.'

'She's with him, isn't she?'

'She might be. She's with him a lot recently.'

'Why didn't you tell me, son? That she's been spending time with him?'

'Like I said, it's nothing to do with me. I've already told her what I think about him.'

Tom looked towards his feet. They were cold against the concrete. He pushed against the door and stepped back inside the house.

'Who is he?' asked Emmett.

Tom shrugged, 'You should talk to Elise about it.'

Emmett stepped forwards and leant on the door with his forearm. 'You tell me now!' he said.

'He's called Jack,' said Tom. 'Jack Clapham.'

'Jack Clapham. The boy who used to live across the street?'

'Yeah, he said he knew you.'

'You've met him?'

'Yeah I met him at The Phonebox.'

'What does he want with Elise?'

'Not a clue.'

'Where does he live?'

'You can't go to his house.'

'Tom.'

'Just talk to Elise about it. She'll stop meeting with him if you ask her.'

'Where does he live?'

'I'm not telling you the address.'

'Where does he live?'

'26 Dreston Road.'

Two Days Later

Emmett drove carefully towards Dreston Road. His fret heightened with each passing car. The uncertainty around Jack Clapham and the burglary at his shop was strangling him. He coughed into his hand and stopped at a traffic light. His need for answers had pulled him to Jack's house. He had been thinking about him. He had been thinking about Grace too. He made the journey to Dreston Road alone, intent on finding a resolution. He continued through the streets. He drove until he saw Dreston Road. He turned right and parked across the road from Number 26. He looked at the house. It was grand and alluring. He stepped from the car and walked across the street. He could hear sounds from inside the house. He knocked on the door loudly.

'Open up you bastard!'

He beat the door with his fist until he heard footsteps coming towards him. He held a stern face, something he had practised over many years. The door opened and behind it stood Elijah with a cigarette in his hand.

'Mr. Rose,' he said. 'You're the last person I expected.'

Emmett stepped forwards from the cold. 'Elijah,' he said. 'What are you doing here? How's your mum?'

Elijah pulled the cigarette. 'She's fine Mr. Rose. What's wrong? You look angry.'

'I'm here to speak to Jack,' he said. 'Tell him to stay away from Elise.'

'Mr. Rose, no. He won't like that.'

'He stays away from her!'

'Mr. Rose, you don't know what he's like!'

'Let me in, son. And stop with the smoking.'

He pulled the cigarette from Elijah's lips and threw it to the floor. 'Let me through,' he continued.

He pushed past Elijah and began walking through the house. He followed the sounds of the television to the door at the end of the hallway. He pushed open the door and walked inside the room. As he did, Jack was already stood.

He smiled. 'Emmett,' he said. 'How are we?'

Emmett maintained a stern look but shook at the ankles. 'I saw you with Elise,' he said.

Elijah walked back into the room and pushed the door closed. Jack lifted his head towards him.

'Get Emmett a drink, will you? Rum, gin, a beer?' he asked.

Emmett waved a stray hand towards Elijah. 'I'm not staying,' he said. 'I have to get back to Elise.'

'Get him a gin,' said Jack. 'Elise likes it, maybe she got it from her grandad.'

Elijah left for the kitchen and returned shortly with a small glass of gin. 'Here you are, Mr. Rose,' he said.

Emmett placed the glass by his feet, 'I told you I'm not staying. I'm just here to tell you to stay away from her.'

Jack began walking around the room. He looked back towards Emmett. 'Do you remember me?' he asked. 'I used to live across the street from you.'

'Yeah, I remember you. I remember your family.'

'And Grace too. I used to live across the street from Grace.'

'How is the old man? Your dad? Still inside, is he?'

'No, he died,' said Jack. 'He was killed.'

'It was always coming,' said Emmett. 'He was trouble. You all were.'

Jack grinned, 'No, you never did like us. My mum always used to say, Emmett, he doesn't like us!'

Jack's face had reddened, and he had started to squirm. 'Sit down,' he said, pointing towards the open chair. 'Please.'

'I'd prefer to stand,' said Emmett.

'Sit,' said Jack. 'If you stand, I have to stand and I'd prefer to sit.'

Emmett held pose for a moment but then buckled. He took the glass of gin from the floor, finished it, and carried the glass with him to the open chair. Jack sat on the settee opposite him.

'You don't look well,' he said. 'You don't look as strong as you used to.'

Emmett placed the glass by his feet. 'Yeah, you've changed as well. Still a Clapham, though,' he said. 'Still got that same look.'

'You stay away from Elise, all right. She wants nothing to do with you.'

Jack took the remote and turned off the television. 'She was the one who came to see me, actually,' he said. 'She sat in that chair and asked for my help.'

'What help would she want from you?'

'Just help.'

'She wants nothing to do with you.'

'Well, maybe you don't know her as well as you think.'

He stood and waved his finger at Jack, 'I'm not here to play your smart games,' he said. 'She's my granddaughter. You fucking keep away.'

'What did I tell you about standing,' said Jack.

Emmett gestured towards the door, 'I'll never let a Clapham near my family. I told Grace to stay away from your lot and I'll tell Elise the same.'

Jack's smile cracked. It seemed that the mention of Grace's name had caused him to tighten his fists. Elijah noticed his fret and tapped him on the shoulder.

'Let him go,' he said.

Jack stood and walked towards Emmett, 'Elise is a woman now. She can do what she wants.'

'You've not changed, have you?' said Emmett. 'Your family. You're all the same, aren't you?'

'Why did we bother you so much?' asked Jack.

'I don't trust you. I don't trust any of you.'

'Elise trusts me.'

'Elise doesn't know you. I'll give you a week to cut ties with her or I'm moving her away. She can go and live with my sister in Scotland.'

'Maybe you should leave,' said Elijah 'Mr. Rose, I think it's for the best.'

Emmett looked at Elijah, who stood restlessly, 'You can do better than this son. You were a good kid. You should spend more time with your mum.'

Emmett pressed his hand on the handle of the door. 'A week,' he said. 'Or she's leaving. I'm not having her ruining her life.'

Jack held his hand sarcastically across his chest, 'You think I'm going to ruin her life. No one's asking her to be here. She's grown now. She's making her own decisions.'

Emmett opened the door and looked back at Jack for a final time. His eyes had become focused. 'Stay away from her,' he said. 'I mean it. You'll have nothing to do with her, I can promise you that.'

He then disappeared along the hallway and left the house. Elijah followed him and then quickly returned to the front room.

'He's gone,' he said. 'He's driving home.'

Jack stood, toiling with Emmett's words. 'He's got some nerve, hasn't he?' he said. 'I'll give him that.'

Elijah walked towards him and passed him a cigarette. 'Stupid old man,' he said.

Jack took the cigarette and smoked it at the back of the house.

'Do you want a drink?' asked Elijah. His voice was quiet and careful.

Jack shook his head. He finished his cigarette and walked up the stairs to his bedroom. He reached his room and closed the door behind him. He placed his hands on the side of his head and pulled them down across his face. He kicked at his bed and curled his hands through his hair. He stopped and stood still. He bit at his fingernails. He became flustered and took off his jacket. He pulled at the sleeves of his shirt. He walked towards his bedroom window and looked out. He pushed his forehead against the window. He stepped back with a pointed face and sweat on his hands.

'I promise,' he said. 'I promise. I promise. I promise.'

'Elise.'

Chapter 10
Behind the Door Stood Two Police Officers

2 Days Later

'Open up!'

'Open up!'

'It's the police.'

'Is there anybody in there?'

'It's about Emmett Rose!'

Elise woke to loud knocks at the front door. She moaned, stepped from bed, walked down the stairs, through the kitchen and opened the door. Behind the door stood two police officers. She squinted with the morning sun. The signs of sleep were still etched on her face.

'Can I help you?' she asked.

The first officer stepped forwards. He was a short man with red hair and had a gold band around his wedding finger.

'Can we come in?' he asked. 'Is this the home of Emmett Rose?'

The second officer was a taller woman with crooked teeth and creases on her forehead. 'Can we?' she asked.

Elise moved aside and gestured for the officers to come in. Both officers smiled nervously as they walked inside the house. Elise closed the door and followed them into the front room.

'Is there a problem?' she asked.

The officers stood with their shoulders touching in the centre of the room.

'We have some difficult news,' said the male officer.

Elise folded her arms and took steps towards the kitchen. 'If this is about the burglary at my grandad's shop,' she said. 'You'll have to come back later. He's already left for work.'

The officers looked nervously at one another. The female officer was persistent with her stare. She widened her eyes and leaned her head forwards.

'Tell her,' she said.

The male officer grimaced and took a half-step forward. 'We have some bad news,' he said. 'Your grandad was attacked last night. He's in hospital. He has some serious injuries.'

'He's been attacked?'

'Someone went for him,' said the female officer.

'Are you winding me up?'

'He has some serious injuries to his head and right leg.'

Elise's body tightened. 'This place,' she said, smiling. 'Fucking-hell.'

She left the room and scurried into the kitchen. She stood with her back to the officers who had followed her from the front room. The male officer came behind her and put his hand across her back. She turned and pushed him away. Her face had reddened and there was a tear on her cheek.

'Who was it?' she asked. 'Was it the people who burgled the shop? Their friends? He told you they'd come for him. He told you he wasn't safe!'

The male officer tried to take her by the arm. 'You need to be strong for your grandad,' he said.

'Fuck off,' she replied. 'Just fuck off, will you?'

She turned away and scratched at the skin on her face. 'Where'd it happen?' she asked.

'A few streets away,' said the female officer. 'He was found last night. Someone saw him from their window. They must've got him walking home.'

'I want to see him,' she said. 'I want to see him now.'

'We can take you to the hospital,' said the male officer. 'We can take you there, but you should probably get dressed first. You can't go to the hospital in your pyjamas.'

Elise looked down at her clothes. 'They're not pyjamas. It's a fucking t-shirt,' she said.

She had blushed. She wiped at her eyes and forehead. 'I'll be five minutes,' she said. 'Just stay here, please.'

She heard more knocks at the front door. 'Elise! Elise!' shouted a voice.

She passed the officers and opened the door. Behind it stood Tom.

'What's with the police car?' he asked. 'Has something happened?'

'Someone's attacked my grandad.'

'Fuck.'

'Yeah, someone got him walking home last night.'

'Where is he?'

'The police are taking me to the hospital now.'

'I'll come with you.'

'I need to get dressed first. You can wait in here. I'll only be five minutes.'

Elise closed the door and ran up the stairs. She dressed and sat for a moment on her bed. She shook her head and stood. She pulled her hair back and tied it in place with a bobble. She slammed her bedroom door shut and walked down the stairs.

'Are you all ready?' she asked.

The officers nodded together and Tom was still waiting by the front door.

'Let's go then,' she said.

She followed the officers from the house and sat in the back of the police car with Tom. She sat biting at her bottom lip. The male officer turned towards them.

'Are you coming too?' he asked.

Tom nodded.

Elise pointed ahead. 'Can we just go?' she asked.

As they drove, the officers started talking between themselves.

'He's milking it,' said the female officer. 'He should be back by now. How far did he fall? 10 feet? He's been off nearly three months!'

'Definitely milking it,' said the male officer.

'Someone should say something,' said the female officer.

'Not worth it.'

'Yeah, you're probably right.'

The hospital was a short drive from Elise's home. The officers drove through the streets, turned the final corner, and parked in the hospital car park.

'Anyway, I'm going to say something to him when he gets back,' said the female officer, as she took off her seatbelt. 'He should've been back weeks ago.'

The male officer stopped the engine, turned towards Elise, and pinched his eyebrows, 'Now, he doesn't look great so prepare yourself.'

'Thanks for the lift,' she said, and left the car. She crossed the car park and soon started running towards the entrance. She pushed past people and through a small crowd. She ran towards the front desk in reception and spoke to a thin man with glasses on his nose.

'Emmett Rose,' she said. 'I need to see Emmett Rose.'

The man pushed the glasses up his nose and pointed forwards.

'There's a queue,' he said.

She leaned across the counter. 'Emmett Rose!' she said.

Another man then approached her. He took her by the shoulder and ushered her away. The man was tall and leant down to speak.

'Who are you?' she asked.

'I'm a doctor at the hospital,' he said. 'And if you don't quiet down, I will have to insist that you leave.'

Tom and the officers quickly followed her into the reception, the officers rushed towards her and started apologising to the doctor.

'Come on Elise,' said the male officer. 'This way. He's in the intensive care unit.'

She turned towards the doctor, 'cunt,' she said.

The male officer walked ahead and guided her through the corridors. As she walked, she noticed the scattered people and mournful looks. There was an instant change in atmosphere;

it was a mixture of all things dark. The male officer pushed through a set of double doors and up a flight of stairs.

'Just this way,' he said.

Elise, Tom, and the female officer followed him to the end of a long corridor. He pushed through a final set of double doors and walked into the intensive care unit. Elise followed the officer to an elongated window at the back of the unit. Behind the window lay her grandfather. He was attached to a ventilation machine. He was led on a bed with tubes pouring from his mouth. His face was bruised, and his right leg was held in place by a brace.

She pressed her head towards the window. 'He doesn't look good,' she said. 'His eyes are shut. He's got cuts all over him.'

Emmett was dressed in a lazy blue gown. There were blankets under his legs and a pillow under his head. The police officers walked towards her.

'We'll give you some time,' said the female officer.

'We'll be over there if you need anything,' said the male officer.

She turned to them and smiled. 'Thanks,' she said.

Tom waited with her. He stood with his hands in his pockets. 'He's alive,' he said. 'It sounds strange, but it could be worse.'

She scratched her head. She stepped back from the window and noticed a man walking towards her. He held a clipboard and wore a white shirt. The man was bald and had noticeably small hands.

'Are you of relation to this man?' he asked.

She turned towards him. 'He's my grandad,' she said.

'I'm Dr Violet. I'll be looking after Emmett while he's with us.'

'He looks terrible.'

'He has a fractured skull and right leg. It's very serious,' he said. 'He has some swelling on the brain. We've had to put him in a coma for now. It's just a precaution.'

'Is he going to die? Just tell me if he is. I'd prefer if you just told me.'

'I don't know. It's a big injury at his age. We'll know more soon.'

Dr Violet quickly ran through his notes and then folded the clipboard to his side. 'There is one thing I'm sure of,' he said.

'What?' asked Elise.

'Whoever did this, they wanted him dead. He's lucky to still have a chance,' he said.

Elise seemed to wilt. 'It was them,' she said. 'The people who burgled the shop. He told the police they'd come for him.'

Dr Violet edged towards her. 'I've been a doctor for nearly 15 years and I still don't know how to react when people get upset,' he said. 'Would you like a hug?'

She shook her head, 'No. Can I see him?'

'No, not yet. He's resting, maybe in a few days.'

'So, what happens now?'

'We wait. We see how he does.'

'That's it?'

'That's it. My advice is to be realistic. Hopeful but realistic.'

Dr Violet nodded towards her. 'Hopeful but realistic,' he repeated and then disappeared along the corridors.

Elise watched as he walked away. 'Did you hear that?' she asked. 'Realistic. Hopeful but realistic. I wanted him to tell me that everything's going to be all right.'

'He can't tell you that.'

'He's a doctor, he should know.'

'Elise,' said a voice from behind. It was the male officer. 'We have to go now. We're needed somewhere else. What did the doctor say?'

'To be realistic.'

'They're looking after him. He's in the best possible hands.'

'Will you be in touch. Let me know if there's any arrests.'

'We will. I will personally, I promise.'

'Thanks. I'm sorry I swore at you, it just, fuck…'

'Don't worry. I'm a police officer, I'm used to it. Be safe all right?'

79

The officers left the unit and Elise returned to the elongated window.

'Fractured skull,' she said. 'Look at him. Look at the cuts on his face.' She winced and hit the window with an open palm.

Tom stood behind her. He watched as she struggled. 'I need to tell you something,' he said. 'Something I should've already told you.'

'What?'

'Emmett came to see me.'

'About what?'

'About Jack.'

'Jack?'

'He saw you with him.'

'He didn't say anything to me.'

'He asked for his address. I think he might've gone to his house.'

'So, you think Jack did this?'

'Emmett comes to see me about Jack Clapham and less than a week later he's in hospital. What do you think?'

'Why would Jack hurt my grandad?'

Tom let out a desperate exhale. 'How much do you know about him? Really? You don't know anything about him. How would you know his reasons for doing anything?'

Elise sensed sincerity in Tom's tone. She pressed towards the window and listened to the rhythmic beats of the ventilation machine as she pondered.

'Jack,' she said.

She looked at her grandfather's corrupted frame, the cuts on his arms, and the marks around his nose. She looked at his room, it was small and desperate.

Tom walked towards her. He pulled at her arm with his hand. 'Elise,' he said, 'Elise, we should go.'

She pushed him away and stepped forwards. She was so close to the window that she could see her breath on the glass.

'Jack?'

Chapter 11
Tight Fists

'It was you!'

'You did it!'

'It was you!'

'Why'd you have to do that?'

'Why'd you have to hurt him?'

She struck Jack on the cheek. She lost control of her facial expressions, curled her hands into fists and hit them against his chest.

'You did this,' she said. 'You hurt him.'

Jack lunged forwards and took her by the arms. He curled his fingers over her skin and pulled her close. She struggled with his hands.

'What's happened?' he asked. 'What's happened? I've never seen you like this.'

She continued to fight with his hands.

'Why're you so mad?' he continued. 'Just speak to me.'

'You attacked my grandad.'

'Has someone attacked him?'

'You fucker.'

'It wasn't me. Why would you think it's me?'

'I know it was you. Don't lie to me.'

Elise started to kick Jack. Elijah leapt forwards and intervened. He wrestled his body in front of her and pushed her back with his arms. His face was tight and pale.

'Relax,' he said. 'Just relax.'

She stopped and took a moment to gather her breath. You could see her protruding lungs from under her t-shirt.

'It was him,' she said, under shallow breath. 'He did it.'

Jack hissed and fixed his misplaced jacket. 'I haven't attacked anyone,' he said. 'And I don't appreciate the accusations.'

'Sit down,' he continued.

'Piss off.'

'So, someone's attacked your grandad and you think it's me?'

'Are you denying it?'

'I just want to know how you've worked it all out?'

He sat on the arm of the settee and touched his cheek. He had a small cut under his eye. He pushed at the blood with his finger and wiped it on his jeans, 'So, go on then. I attacked him. Explain it to me.'

'Tom told me that my grandad came to see him.'

'Yeah.'

'He asked for your address.'

'Yeah, he came here.'

'He came here?'

'Yeah, he sat in that chair right there.'

'What did he say?'

'He told me to stay away from you.'

'And what did you say?'

'No.'

'That's it?'

'That's it. He came here about a week ago. I haven't seen him since.'

She pushed forwards from the door. She walked past Elijah and sat down in the open chair. 'You might've been angry, mad that he told you to stay away from me.'

Jack smiled, 'I'll tell you what I told him. There's nobody keeping you here. If you want to leave, fucking leave all right.'

'When did the attack happen, last night?' asked Elijah.

'Yeah.'

'He was with me all night.'

'Are you lying to me, Elijah?'

'He was here all night. Neither of us left.'

'Not for a moment?'

'Emmett was good to me. I wouldn't let anyone hurt him. You know that.'

'You might let Jack.'

'No one, not a soul on this earth.'

She sat and pinched at the skin on her thigh. She was volatile and slightly out of breath. 'If you're lying to me,' she said. 'Both of you, I'll kill you.'

'If you really thought it was me, you would've gone to the police,' said Jack. 'You wouldn't have come here.'

'It doesn't make sense,' said Elijah.

'Do you promise me, Elijah?'

'I promise you.'

She maintained stare with Jack. His face was innocent and marred by a small cut under his eye.

'I didn't mean to do that,' she said. 'I'm going to cut my nails when I get home. That was an accident.'

'Ah, fuck it,' he said.

'Have you been to the hospital?' asked Elijah.

'Yeah, he's a mess.'

'Is he stable?'

'Fractured skull, broken leg. His face is a mess. I don't think stable's the right word.'

Elise lent a hand towards Jack. 'Can I have a cigarette please?' she asked.

'You don't smoke?' he replied.

She shrugged, 'That's what people do, isn't it? When they're stressed, they have a cigarette.'

Elijah gestured towards his jacket pocket, but Jack snapped and grabbed him by the wrist. 'You're not having one,' he said. 'It's a bad habit. I wish I never started.'

Elise snarled. 'Just give me one,' she said. 'Stop being a knob.'

Jack sat back and pouted his lips. 'No,' he said. 'What did the doctors say, specifically?'

'He has swelling on the brain.'

'Is he in a coma?' asked Elijah.

'Yeah, how'd you know?'

'They did the same to my uncle Des after his car accident.'

'It's scary.'

'I know.'

'What's your uncle Des doing now?'

'He lives in Spain. He's happy.'

Elijah noticed her discomfort and left the room. He returned from the kitchen shortly with three glasses, two filled with rum and one with gin. He smiled and passed the gin to Elise.

'You look like you could do with a drink,' he said.

She took a sip. 'It was the people who burgled his shop,' she said. 'It has to be, their friends or family.'

'You thought it was me a minute ago,' said Jack. 'You were convinced.'

'Well, now it's them. I'm convinced.'

'Are you talking about the note?' asked Jack.

'What note?' asked Elijah.

'He had a note under the door of the shop, telling him to drop the charges.'

'Did he show it to the police?' asked Elijah.

'They told him not to worry about it. Idle threats, they called it.'

Jack let out an exasperated moan and turned the glass of rum in his hands. 'Police,' he said. 'You can't trust them to tie their own shoelaces.'

He crossed one leg over the other and rested the glass on his knee. 'We'll ask around,' he said. 'See if anyone knows anything. You can't go around beating up old men. It's not right.'

Elise took a long and depressing sip. 'Why him?' she asked. 'Why couldn't it have been someone else?'

'It's bad for anyone,' said Elijah.

'But why him? He's had enough me, Mum.'

'He's strong enough.'

'Can we go out?' she asked. 'The Phonebox or something?'

'Out?'

'I need to get out of this room for a bit. It's too hot. Can you turn the heating down?'

'Yeah. I'll turn it down, but relax. Whoever it was, they'll be caught eventually.'

'Yeah.'

'Enjoy your gin.'

'Yeah, it's actually pretty good.'

As she sat, she pictured her grandfather in hospital. With the tubes in his mouth and the scrapes on his skin. She winced and took another sip. She thought about the sentiments of Dr Violet, "be realistic". The words felt like a cold slap in the face. As she thought, she could feel Jack watching her. Even as he spoke with Elijah, she could feel his stare on her skin. She soon felt a rush of guilt. Even in her mania, she knew he was innocent.

'Sorry,' she said. 'I shouldn't have blamed you.'

He smiled. 'You were angry,' he said. 'Don't worry about it.'

She held his stare with tears in her eyes. 'The doctors don't think he'll make it. Be realistic, they said. Realistic.'

'He's still kicking, isn't he?'

'Yeah.'

'It's a shame,' said Elijah. 'Bad timing.'

'Bad timing?' said Elise.

'Yeah, Jack was going to tell you about the job.'

'Not now!' said Jack.

'What?' said Elijah. 'Am I lying?'

'It's not the time,' he replied.

Elijah brooded and pulled out his packet of cigarettes.

'You were going to tell me about the job?' asked Elise. 'Have you spoken to Frankie? Did he say I could be involved?'

'Yeah, I spoke to him. He was reluctant, but he agreed.'

'So, you can tell me about it?'

'Yeah, but it's not the time. It can wait.'

'Tell me. I want to know.'

Elijah took a drag of his cigarette and passed it to Jack. He shrugged. 'Tell her,' he said. 'She wants to know. Tell her.'

Jack took the cigarette and held it between his fingers. He leant forwards and took an ashtray from the carpet. He seemed to half-smile.

'There's this family,' he said. 'This family lives in a big house. They have nice things. They buy each other expensive gifts, you know.'

'We have a tip that they're going away soon,' he continued. 'To a winter wedding in Spain. It sounds lovely, actually.'

'So, we burgle them?' asked Elise.

'Ha-ha,' said Elijah.

'The house will be empty,' said Jack. 'It would be a shame not to.'

'Who gave you this tip?'

'Don't worry. We can trust him.'

'Why do you need me?'

'We don't. The job could be done with two people.'

Jack smiled widely, exposing teeth and gums. 'This is it,' he said. 'This is for you. This is the chance you need to take.'

She took a sip of gin. She rested the glass against her bottom lip. 'A burglary,' she said. 'Fucking-hell, where am I?'

As she sat, she once again thought of her grandfather. He felt distant and the gap between them troubled her. Even in her times of madness, she could still feel him beside her. She longed for his spirit. She raised her head and looked at Jack. He was sat, purring, 'So, are you in?' he asked.

Chapter 12
Crayons

She sat on the fence facing Darcy Lane, her legs hung, and her hands held onto a piece of plain white paper. Beside her, on the fence, sat a selection of crayons. She was alone, but in fine company. She rested joyfully with the house, pond, and grass. She sat scribbling the shape of the house onto the paper. Her hands were tense, she cared over each line and each scrape of the crayon. Even when the wind picked up and curled around her neck, even when the day became cold, she maintained her dedication to the drawing. She picked up the red crayon and started to draw with it. She drew the front door of the house. Over time, she passed each crayon through her hands. She warmed as she drew. She took the blue crayon and flooded the page with deep puddles. She drew the pond and coloured it in. She smiled and looked out towards the house.

She held up the paper. 'The pond,' she said to herself, and returned the paper to her lap. She had escaped to Darcy Lane. Her first job with Jack was approaching and her nerves could not settle. She was not sleeping. She had stopped taking her medication too. The daze it gave her had become insufferable and she disposed of the pills each morning as she brushed her teeth. She would throw the pills down the sink and wash them away with water and toothpaste. Despite her concerns, she had still not agreed to be a part of the job.

Jack had been understanding, he always was. 'Take your time,' he said, 'you don't need to make a decision straight away.'

Elise made the finishing touches to her drawing. She placed the crayons on the fence beside her and held the paper in front of her face.

She smiled youthfully. 'Nearly there,' she said. She took the red crayon for a final time and placed the paper on her lap. *Property of Elise Rose*, she wrote in the bottom corner of the page. She then took the paper, folded it twice and placed it into the pocket of her jeans. Before her morning of artistry, she had first visited her grandfather at the hospital. She woke early, scratched through the streets, and waited patiently outside his room. At the hospital, she was struck with the same uneasy feeling. She waited by the window and looked for signs of improvement. She was soon joined by Dr Violet. He had shaved since she last saw him.

'You've shaved,' she said.

'Yes,' he replied. 'I have.'

'How is he?'

'It's the same story.'

'That sounds like bad news.'

'For a man of his age, it's actually a positive sign.'

'Do you promise?'

'I promise. Have the police been in touch?'

'No arrests yet.'

'Damn.'

'No, I don't think they're any closer.'

'Well, on a positive note, you can see him now if you want.'

'Go in the room?'

'Yeah.'

Dr Violet walked around her and pressed against the door of Emmett's room. 'Come on,' he said. 'I'll come in with you.'

She took an instinctive half-step backwards. She peered towards her grandfather's stricken figure.

'Not yet,' she said. 'I can't go in there yet.'

'I thought you wanted to?'

'It's bad enough from here.'

'Are you sure?'

'Yeah, just for now.'

Dr Violet took his hand from the door. 'Well,' he said. 'You must let me know if you change your mind.'

'I will,' said Elise. 'Thanks.'

'Are you sure you're okay? You look tired. Have you been sleeping?' asked Dr Violet.

'Not really. The house seems big without him.'

'You must look after yourself.'

'I know. I'll get some sleep tonight.'

Dr Violet nodded and scurried from sight. As he walked, accusations of cowardice enveloped her mind. She did want to see her grandfather, touch him even, but standing beside him was something she was not ready for. She stayed at the window for a while longer and then left through the corridors. She had begun to loathe her visits to the hospital. She ran through the streets and towards home.

At home, she pulled a piece of paper from a notepad, collected some old crayons, and retreated to Darcy Lane. Her home at Hirst Street had become too quiet without her grandfather. She had tried to fill her days. She worked at the shop and spent time between the streets, but the emptiness of home had become painful.

At night-time, she had even resorted to reading from her mother's journal to pass time. She focused on the earlier entries, reading and rereading passages about her grandfather as a younger man. She recognised him from her mother's words. He had not changed. He still had the same stoic intent; the same stern demeanour. However, it also showed a man who was content with his life. He was happily married and resolved to raising a young daughter to the best of his abilities.

Emmett was once married to a lady called Fran. Her full name was Francesca, but from the entries in the journal, it seemed she was rarely called by her proper name. Fran was Grace's mother. She shared a sincere relationship with Emmett, one that was reasonable and often fulfilling. Emmett had once worked as a teacher at the local school and Francesca worked as a waitress at a nearby restaurant.

They were comfortable together and had been married since Emmett was 25 and Francesca 24. They met at a local dance. It was nothing extraordinary, but meaningful to them. She was energetic, joyful, and funny. He was mature, dependable, and moral. They found a house, and Fran soon gave birth to a young girl. They called her Grace. Grace's upbringing was normal. She was quiet and studious. She liked to draw and eat sweets.

On Sundays, when Emmett would leave for a day with his friends at the cricket club, Fran and Grace would sit, listen to Fran's old music, and draw whatever their imaginations could create. Fran died when Grace was 21. The death was sudden and unexpected. It was at this time when the entries in the journal started to darken.

After Fran's death, Emmett and Grace moved from the house and onto the estate. Emmett rarely spoke of Fran. He hid his pictures of her in cabinets and threw away many of her old drawings. Grace now had Sunday mornings to herself and instead of drawing, she started to spend time between the streets. Emmett soon left his job as a teacher and used the rest of his money to buy the shop. He soon started to spend all of his time at the shop and Grace, now 21 and untarnished, started to find comfort in others.

Elise stayed at Darcy Lane for a while longer. She was happy beside the house, but the thoughts of the forthcoming burglary still worried her. She could not sit still or help but picture the family she would be stealing from. She soon left the fence and walked back along the path. She waited by the bus stop until she saw the Number 12 bus coming towards her. She stretched out her arm and waited for the bus to stop. She smiled at the bus driver upon arrival.

'What do you do here?' he asked.

Elise simply smiled and walked towards the back of the bus, still unsure of her next steps.

Chapter 13
Neck Deep

Two Weeks Later

Jack stood with an outstretched arm. 'Hurry up and pour it,' he said.

Elise also stood with her arm outstretched, clasping a small glass of gin, and casting a strained figure. She pulled the glass towards her and took a quick sip.

'Sorry,' she said. 'I couldn't wait.'

Frankie waited patiently. He stood, turning a half-smoked cigarette in his fingers, and holding a glass of rum in his hand. Frankie had become quiet. He was rarely a man who sought attention, but he was even quieter than usual. He was smoking more than he usually did and drinking a little less. He stood with his head hung, he took a short sip and flared his nostrils.

Elijah stood struggling with the bottle of rum. He finally loosened the cap and poured his glass.

'Finally,' he said. 'I had sweaty hands. I must be nervous.'

Jack smiled lavishly. 'At last,' he said. 'Wipe your hands, son. It's time for a toast.'

'I'll leave it to you,' said Frankie.

'Good,' said Jack. 'I'll say a few words.'

Jack stepped forwards and raised his glass a little higher. 'Raise them,' he said. 'Raise your glasses.'

Elijah raised his glass and Frankie held out a slumbering arm.

'Higher than that,' he said. 'Tonight's the night.' he continued. 'Higher than that.'

Frankie smiled and raised his glass a little higher. As he did, Elise noticed cracks in his usually tough demeanour.

Jack made a deliberate look towards Elijah. 'We want no problems tonight,' he said. 'We're in and out in five minutes. Clean, that's the operative word. Clean – a clean job.'

'Now,' he continued, with a handsome grin. 'This is Elise's first job, an important occasion in the life of any young thief! So first we toast to Elise. To Elise!'

'To Elise!'

Each man then finished his drink. Elise pondered over her glass. 'I'm not good at downing drinks,' she said. 'I'll take a sip.'

'Finish it,' said Frankie. 'It'll do you good.'

She sensed sincerity in his voice and finished her drink. Jack and Elijah stood laughing.

'Fill them again,' said Jack. 'Don't worry, Elise. This is the last one.'

Each glass was then refilled, three with rum and one with gin. As he poured rum, Elise could see frivolity in Jack's movements. He was at ease, as though he had found meaning amongst the madness. He passed the bottle of rum to Elijah and started walking around the room.

'We all know the plan,' he said. 'Frankie and Elijah, you take downstairs. Me and Elise will take upstairs. We all know about the cars. They'll be two of them. If we can get into them, Frankie and Elijah you take them. If we can't, well, we'll have to make do with what's in the house.'

'Yeah, sweet,' said Frankie.

'Elise, me and you, we have the upstairs. I've told you what we're after. Jewellery is the priority. After that we can get creative, but jewellery is the priority. A family like this, they might have a safe too, but I don't know how to break safes, so we'll have to leave it.'

'What about the security cameras?'

'There's one at the front of the house but it won't be a problem. Elijah, if you can reach it then break it, but it's not important. Just keep your balaclava's on at all times, even in the house. We'll be fine as long as nobody shows their face.'

'What about an alarm?'

'Maybe, maybe not. A family like this, there could be, but it changes nothing. Either way, we're gone before the police have left the station,'

'Perfect,' said Frankie.

'Everybody happy?'

'Happy.'

'Happy.'

'Happy.'

Jack stretched out his arm for a final time. 'Let's all get home safe,' he said. 'Now drink up. It's time to go.'

This time Elise did not hesitate. She finished her drink and left the glass by her feet. She followed Jack from the house and sat in the back of the car with Elijah. Jack drove, and Frankie sat restlessly in the passenger's seat. Each person was dressed in full black clothing.

'Show time,' said Elijah, as he pulled the seatbelt across his body.

Frankie lowered the window on his side and began to smoke. 'When did you pick up the car?' he asked.

'Last night,' replied Jack.

'Are you taking it back after?'

'Yeah. Same as last time.'

Jack pulled out of the driveway and onto the street. He was precise in his movements, as though he had become focused and aware. The drive was largely silent. Jack and Frankie smoked, while Elise and Elijah looked sparingly from the windows.

'You two are quiet,' said Jack, eventually. 'Anyone would think you're nervous.'

'Are you not?' asked Elise.

'No.'

'Are you, Frankie?'

'No, relax. Five minutes. In and out in five minutes.'

The streets were quiet too. It was late, and the winter's cold had ushered many of the locals inside.

Jack drove and peered out from over the steering wheel. 'Beautiful night,' he said. 'Really nice.'

Frankie opened the glovebox and took out four black balaclavas and four pairs of leather gloves. He sorted them in his hands and passed a balaclava and a pair of gloves to each person.

'Don't put the balaclava on yet,' he said, leaning his head towards Elise. 'We'll tell you when.'

Elise pulled the gloves over her hands and clenched her fists.

'Professional,' she said.

Jack turned. 'We don't mess around,' he said. 'Gloves are essential.'

'How far?' asked Elijah.

'Five minutes.'

'My heart's going,' said Elise.

'Do you want a cigarette?'

'No, I'm fine.'

The car rolled onwards. Elise watched as Jack pulled the gloves over his hands. His movements seemed so natural. He pulled the gloves tight and then returned his hands to the steering wheel. He started to listen to music from the radio. It was classical and surprising.

'A little superstition,' he said. 'It's always classical music before a job.'

'Why?'

'My mum loved classical music and so do I.'

Frankie coughed into his gloves and pointed forwards. 'Just up there,' he said.

Jack ducked his head and sat forwards in his seat. 'Yeah, we're close,' he said. 'Balaclavas on.'

Elise stretched the dark fabric over her head and pulled it down across her face. She watched from the window as Jack pulled the car around the final corner.

'This is the road,' he said. 'Everyone, get ready.'

They drove carefully along the street. 'Which one?' asked Elijah.

'Two from the end,' said Jack. 'Just a little further.'

Elise watched as they passed each house. She waited until the car started to slow and then undid her seatbelt. Jack pointed forwards. You could see the smile from under his balaclava.

'It's that one,' he said. 'The one with the black door.'

Jack drove towards the house and rolled the car quietly onto the driveway. He stopped the car and immediately opened the door.

'We go in through the back,' he said. 'Come on.'

Each person then stepped from the car. Jack walked towards the boot, opened it, and pulled out a crowbar and a pair of bolt cutters. He passed the crowbar to Frankie and the pair of bolt cutters to Elijah.

'Move!' he said.

'What about the camera? I think I can reach it.'

'Forget it.'

Elijah walked towards the gate at the side of the house and climbed over it. He broke the lock with the bolt cutters and pulled the gate open. Frankie was the first to rush through. He ran along the side of the house and instantly started working on the back door. He struggled for a moment, but the door soon opened.

'These doors are getting stronger,' he said. 'Or maybe I'm just getting weaker.'

Jack pushed the door open and walked inside the house. He strolled through the back of the house and towards the kitchen. Elise, Elijah, and Frankie followed behind.

'There's car keys here,' he said, as he reached the kitchen. 'Frankie and Elijah, you take the car. See if you can get into the other one too. If not, just take this one.'

'What about downstairs?' asked Frankie.

'Don't worry about it. That's a £90,000 car, that. Why would they just leave the keys here?'

'Come on,' said Frankie.

'You know where you're taking it, don't you?' asked Jack.

'Yeah, yeah. Come on, Elijah.'

Frankie took the keys and rushed towards the garage at the front of the house.

'There's no alarm,' said Elise.

'No,' said Jack. 'I thought there would be.'

Jack moved through the kitchen and towards the stairs. He climbed them at a pace. Elise followed behind. She walked until she was stopped by violent screams. She paused at the bottom of the stairs. She could hear a woman's voice. She climbed the stairs and followed the screams. She walked into one of the bedrooms to see Jack clambering over a woman's figure.

'No names!' he shouted. 'No names!'

'Stop!' he said. 'Stop fighting!'

'Get something to tie her with,' he continued.

'To tie her with?' asked Elise.

'Yeah!'

'I thought the house was supposed to be empty.'

'Just fucking go!'

Elise ran downstairs. She ran towards the kitchen and frantically started searching in the draws and cupboards. 'There's nothing here!' she shouted. 'I can't find anything!'

She ran towards the garage. Frankie, Elijah, and one of the cars had already gone. She started rummaging around on the floor and in boxes. She fumbled through the boxes until she found a roll of tape and two old skipping ropes. She took them in hand and rushed back up the stairs. She passed them to Jack who had forced the woman to the ground.

'Skipping ropes?' he said. 'Fucking skipping ropes?'

Jack took the ropes and started to tie the woman to the foot of the bed. He pulled the ropes around her stomach and tied them between the gaps in the wooden frame. The woman was screaming. Elise had heard screaming before, from fallen children and on television, but this was different.

She was unsure if the woman even knew that she was screaming. The screams were too violent and uncontrolled to be established in conscious thought.

'Cover her mouth,' said Jack, 'while I do this. Quickly.'

Elise leant forwards and stretched her hands over the woman's mouth. As she did, their eyes caught for a moment and Elise became breathless. Jack took the roll of tape and used it to tie the woman's hands behind her back. He then took the tape, wrapped it around the woman's torso and secured it around the frame of the bed.

'She's not getting out of that any time soon,' he said. 'Good work with the skipping ropes.'

He stood and moaned. 'Fuck,' he said. 'It was supposed to be empty.'

Elise still had her hands over the woman's mouth. 'She's licking my hand,' she said. 'What should I do?'

Jack walked towards the head of the bed and pulled a pillow from the mattress. He removed the pillowcase and knelt down beside her.

'Move your hands,' he said.

Jack took the pillowcase, wrapped it around the woman's mouth and tied it tightly at the back of her head. He then took the woman by the cheeks.

'Is there anybody else in the house?' he asked. 'Shake or nod.'

The woman shook her head.

'Good,' he said. 'Now tell us where the jewellery is, and we'll leave, okay? It's as easy as that. You tell us, we leave.'

He started to pull at the pillowcase. 'I'm going to lower this,' he said. 'And you're not going to scream. Shake or nod.'

The woman nodded her head and Jack pulled the pillowcase from her mouth.

'It's all in there,' she said. 'The top drawer of the dressing table.'

'Check,' said Jack.

Elise walked towards the dressing table and opened the top drawer. Inside, there was a large wooden jewellery box.

'Bring it here,' he said.

She took the box and passed it to Jack. He opened it, examined the contents and then passed it back to Elise.

'Something else,' he said. 'More. We need more.'

'You said you'd leave if I told you.'

'We will, but there has to be more.'

'There's plenty in that box.'

'We need more.'

'There isn't any more!'

Jack fumed and punched the woman in the ribs. 'Don't be fucking stupid,' he said. 'Just tell us and we'll leave.'

The woman folded with the punch and looked towards a large wooden wardrobe at the side of the room. 'My husband has watches,' she said. 'He keeps them in there. In the bottom drawer, on the left.'

'Check.'

Elise opened the drawer, and once again there was a large wooden box inside. She took it and passed it to Jack. He opened it, gleefully. Inside, there was a selection of watches – some gold, some silver and some a little more discreet.

'Perfect,' he said. 'Now, we'll leave.'

'Are you going to untie me?'

'No.'

He rested the box by his knees and pulled the pillowcase back over the woman's mouth. He then took the tape and used it to tighten the pillowcase around her head.

'Are we just going to leave her?' asked Elise.

'Yeah,' said Jack. 'Come on, let's go.'

Jack stood and picked the wooden box from the floor. 'Pass me the other one,' he said.

Elise passed him the jewellery box and followed him from the house. They ran from the back door, through the gate, along the driveway and past the wide-open garage door.

'Only one,' he said, as he ran towards the car. 'Fuck, we only got one.'

He put the boxes in the boot, rushed to his side of the car and sat behind the wheel. Elise hurried to the passenger's seat. She was trembling and panting for breath. They started the car and drove away from the house.

'What a drama that was,' he said. 'I don't think she was happy to see us.'

'I thought the house was supposed to be empty!' said Elise.

'Yeah, it was,'

'You and your tips.'

'Don't worry, he's just lost half of his cut.'

She regained her breath and took off her balaclava.

'Keep it on,' said Jack.

Elise shook her head. 'It's too hot,' she replied. 'I can't keep it on.'

Jack drove thoughtfully. 'Yeah, you're right,' he said, and pulled off his balaclava. He turned the corner and sped up along the open road.

Elise ran her hands through her hair. 'Did you see her face?' she asked. 'The woman? I've only ever seen a face like that once before.'

Jack removed his gloves and threw them down towards his feet. He had a small blemish on his knuckles. He held them towards his mouth and sucked on them.

'It's called shock,' he said. 'They all make it. It's the same face every time.'

'So, what now?' she asked.

'I want to take you somewhere.'

'Where?'

'I want to take you to Darcy Lane.'

'What, now? We can't go there now. Are you stupid?'

'No, I'm not stupid.'

'Do you really want to go?'

'Yeah.'

'Won't the police be looking for us?'

'No, she won't be getting out of those ties. And anyway, we won't stay for long.'

'Are you sure we shouldn't just get off the streets?'

'Don't worry. We have time.'

Jack drove until the view became familiar.

'Are you sure about this?' asked Elise.

'Yes,' said Jack. 'Don't you want to go?'

She shrugged, 'I'd prefer to get off the roads, honestly. We can go to Darcy Lane tomorrow, after work.'

He massaged his cheek with his fingers. 'Let's go for a little while,' he said. 'We'll be quick, I promise.'

As they drove, Elise tried to rid the picture of the woman's face from her mind. Behind her, she could hear the wooden boxes sliding across the boot. She became riddled with guilt.

In contrary, Jack was buoyant. He was grinning erratically and smoking from the window. He reached out a hand and nudged her on the shoulder.

'Why're you so quiet?' he asked. 'It was good. We got the car, the jewellery, the watches.'

She sat up. 'Maybe we should've just left with the car,' she said. 'Then we wouldn't have had to tie her up.'

Jack smiled. 'Don't be so soft,' he said.

She watched as green stretches appeared before her. Soon, she could see Darcy Lane in the distance. Despite her guilt, she could not help but smile. Jack drove, turned at the path and stopped outside the house.

'Back to paradise,' he said, smiling.

He sat, with a grin etched onto his face. He killed the engine and let out a deliberate exhale.

'Some night,' he said. 'Quite exciting, really.'

Elise was still uneasy. Her hands were shaking, and her feet tapped nervously on the floor.

He smiled towards her. 'Don't worry,' he said. 'No one's looking for us.'

'Why're we here?' she asked.

'Because this place is important,' he replied.

'Yeah, but why now?'

'Do me a favour. Answer me something?'

'Okay.'

'Tell me your favourite thing about this house.'

'My favourite thing? I don't know.'

'Go on. Think, please.'

'I suppose the freedom.'

'Freedom. Exactly, that's what it is. Freedom.'

'Yeah, it's freedom for me.'

'Yeah, freedom.'

'Yeah, but that still doesn't explain why you brought me here.'

Jack held stare with Elise. He hesitated for a moment and then leaned across to kiss her. Their lips touched for a moment and then she pulled away, sharply.

'What are you doing?' she asked. 'Are you fucking joking?'

She pushed back against the car door. She scrambled to undo her seatbelt and then leapt from the car. He tried to stop her, but she pushed away his hands. She started walking away from the car and along the path. He shot from the car and followed her. His face had reddened and he was fumbling his words.

'Elise!' he said. 'Hold on! Hold on!'

'You just tried to kiss me.'

'Yeah.'

'Is that why you brought me here? So, you can kiss me? Fuck me? What?'

'No, I just wanted to bring you here.'

'Are you stupid?'

'No, no, I'm not stupid.'

'Am I supposed to just run into your arms? What, we burgle a house together and just ride off into the sunset. Is that it?'

'I just thought…'

'Thought what? You're twice my age, you prick.'

He blushed. 'Are you making fun now?' he asked.

'You're the same as her!' he continued. 'You're the same as your mum. She could never see a good thing either.'

He curled his hands into fists. He walked towards her and pulled her close.

'What?' she said, smiling. 'Are you going to hit me?'

He snarled and pushed her away. He laughed and started walking back towards the car.

'Where are you going?' she asked.

He turned. 'You're the same as her!' he repeated. 'You're both blind to me!'

He opened the car door, slammed it shut and sat behind the wheel. He started the engine and the wayward sounds tainted the quietened night. He turned the car and drove away along the path.

'Are you just going to leave me here?' she shouted, as the car drove past.

'It's fucking freezing!' she continued. 'You can't just leave me here!'

'Jack! Wait! Jack!'

Chapter 14
Burning Letters

Jack stood menacing over a flame. He stood in his garden, beside a warming bin, throwing the final scraps of paper onto the fire. The bin was old and had often been used to burn shoes and clothes. However, on this night, the bin was used to burn letters and scribbles of misplaced affection.

The letters had been sacred to Jack. He had been collecting them since the age of seventeen. He had kept them safe over the years, with many of the letters still in fine condition. He hid them in wardrobes and read them often. Despite the years of commitment, on this night, the letters curled under heat. Each letter had been written with the utmost care. He had sweltered over each word and pondered over each sentence. Each letter was addressed to the same person, Grace Rose.

Jack had written his first letter to Grace just after his 17th birthday. It was during an afternoon in the summertime when the obsession began. Grace had been on his mind and he escaped to his bedroom, intent on expressing his feelings in paper and ink. Jack, a thin and slim seventeen-year-old boy, pulled a scrap of paper from the side of his room and started writing. He wrote the letter and signed his name at the bottom of the page.

Please write back.
Jack Clapham.

He continued to write to Grace over the years. But despite his obvious affection, he never sent her any of the letters.

Instead, he kept them safe in boxes and hid them in wardrobes. He writhed and threw some of the letters onto the fire. He was angry and embarrassed about his attempt to kiss Elise.

In his frustration, he took the letters from his wardrobe, collected them in his hands, sparked a flame and acted without proper thought. After the death of Grace Rose, Jack mourned her loss and the letters stopped for a short while. Instead, he visited her grave and thought about her often. He took the final handful of letters and threw them onto the fire. He watched as the final scraps of paper wilted under the heat.

He then returned to his house and took the picture of the man and the woman from the wall. He carried the picture outside and held it for a moment in his hands. He broke the glass frame with a large rock, removed the picture and threw it onto the fire. He then threw the beaten frame aside and waited for the flames to subside. He smoked and drank. His mind wandered and darkened until he heard the front door to his house open and shut. He peered nervously through the window but smiled when he saw Elijah coming towards him.

'Jack, it's me.'

'Back here.'

'What happened to the picture in the front room?'

'Burned it. Where's Frankie?'

'Why'd you burn it?'

'I didn't want it. Where's Frankie?'

'He said he's staying out of town for a while.'

'He's not still worried about that woman, is he? Tell him to relax.'

'Yeah, he'll calm down.'

Elijah stood beside Jack and peered down towards the bin. 'Been having a fire, have you?' he asked.

Jack walked towards the bin and placed on the lid. 'Yeah,' he said. 'Just burning some old papers. Nothing important.'

As they spoke, smoke lingered in the air. Elijah stepped back and dabbed at his jacket.

'There must've been a lot of papers,' he said.

Jack smiled. 'Well, not anymore,' he replied. 'Anyway, I thought you were at the shop.'

'I closed up early.'

'I didn't say you could.'

'Well, there's something I need to talk to you about.'

'What?'

'I went to see my mum last night, just for a chat.'

'Yeah.'

'She told me that Emmett's waking up.'

'I thought the doctors weren't hopeful.'

'No, he's waking up.'

Jack's body tensed with the news. 'Are you sure?' he asked. 'I thought he wasn't doing well.'

He pulled his cigarettes from his pocket. 'Do you want a cigarette?' he asked.

'No, I have some,' replied Elijah.

Jack took a cigarette and held it in his hands. 'So, he's getting better,' he said. 'Elise must be happy.'

He rolled the cigarette in his fingers and then pushed it between his lips. He glanced anxiously towards Elijah, who was stood, watching him. He wiped his nose and looked skywards.

'You look like you want to say something,' he said.

Elijah walked tentatively towards him. He was squirming, and his complexion had changed. He took another half-step forward and started to mumble.

'That night,' he said. 'You left the house, didn't you?'

Jack turned and smiled. He took a drag of his cigarette and then looked down towards his feet.

'The night Emmett was attacked, you mean?'

Elijah shook his head. He was visibly distressed.

'You thought I was asleep, didn't you?' he said. 'But I saw you. I saw you come back. You had blood on your jacket.'

Elijah stood, watching Jack's movements. His eyes were frantic and his hands were primed and ready to defend himself. Jack turned.

'Why're you clenching your fists?' he asked. 'Going to hit me, are you?'

'No, I just know what you're like.'

'You're accusing me.'

'Don't fucking lie to me. I know it was you.'

'Why didn't you say anything, then?'

'Because I was thinking.'

'Really?'

'I was trying to think of a way out.'

'It wasn't me.'

'Did he see it was you? That's what's important, that's all that matters – does he know?'

Jack took a drag of his cigarette. 'Go inside,' he said. 'I can't talk out here.'

Elijah held a defiant stare. 'Answer my question,' he said.

Jack turned and faced him. 'Go inside,' he said. 'Do you really think I can talk about it out here?'

Elijah spun and looked around at the nearby houses. 'There's nobody here,' he said. 'There's nobody listening.'

Jack pointed towards the house. 'Just go inside,' he said.

Jack walked towards the bin, folded his sleeves over his hands and carried the bin to the side of the garden. As he did, his face wore signs of sadness. The letters had been more than just scribbles on a page. He looked over his shoulder and gestured towards the house.

'Just go inside!' he said. 'We need to talk.'

He left the bin at the side of the garden and followed Elijah into the house. He stopped at the kitchen and poured himself a small glass of rum. He finished it quickly and poured himself another.

'Rum?' he asked.

'No,' said Elijah, from the front room.

Jack walked into the front room and grimaced with the sight of the empty wall. He had fawned over the picture for many years. The wall seemed naked without it. He walked towards the wall, stared longingly, and took a short sip of rum.

'Nearly six years I've had that picture,' he said. 'Maybe seven.'

'It was nice,' said Elijah. 'Strange, but nice.'

'Yeah, it was, but things end, don't they?'

He sat down in the open chair and rested his arm against the fabric. He let his head fall backwards and held on tightly to his glass. He still held his cigarette between his fingers. As he sat, ash fell onto the carpet below. He sat forwards and took a long sip of rum. As he did, it was noticeable that his skin had become blushed.

'So, you saw me, did you?' he asked. 'All covered in blood?'

'That night, yes.'

'It's the anger,' he said. 'It's always been the anger.'

'Will you be honest?'

'Yeah, I'll be honest. It was me. I attacked him.'

Elijah sat down on the settee and leaned forwards towards him. His hands were still firmly clenched.

'You can't go for him again,' he said. 'I mean it. You have to promise me.'

Jack smiled, 'Are you making the orders now?'

'Emmett was good to me. He looked after me when I was a kid. I won't have you hurting him.'

'I'm good to you.'

'Promise me,' said Elijah. 'Promise me or I'm leaving.'

Jack watched Elijah carefully. His usual joviality had faded, and his eyes had become stern.

'Yeah,' he said. 'I promise. Last time was a mistake.'

Jack seemed to curl with the words and the agony brought him to his feet. He finished his rum and put the empty glass on the mantelpiece. He then pulled an ashtray from the floor and crushed his cigarette under the weight of his fingers.

'How'd it get to this?' asked Elijah.

Jack stood with his back turned. 'Scotland is a long way away,' he said. 'A real long way.'

As he stood, small plumes of smoke crept over his shoulder. His usually loose frame seemed brittle. It was as though his jacket had become too heavy for his shoulders and his knees had become uneasy under the weight of his body. He reached into his pocket and took out another cigarette. He was smiling and talking to himself from under his breath.

Elijah became timid. He stood from the settee, walked towards him, and placed a hand on his shoulder. From where

107

he stood, he could not see Jack's face, but he was sure that it was torn.

Elijah spoke softly, as though careful not to startle or enrage. 'Just tell me,' he said. 'Did he see it was you?'

Jack lit his cigarette and let out a diabolical smirk. 'Yeah,' he said. 'He knows it was me.'

Chapter 15
Three Rings

'Close.'

'You haven't got one yet.'

'You do it, then.'

'I've already got one. This is for two.'

'Please.'

'There you go. That's two.'

Tom and Elise sat isolated from town, in their usual place, on the fence facing Darcy Lane. They sat, throwing stones into a metal bucket they had found at the back of the house. Their visits to Darcy Lane had become routine. Tom had tried to stop arguing and instead, thought of ways to entertain himself while at the house. Elise's morning had been dull. Emmett was still in the hospital and the house remained quiet without him. She soon became restless and knocked on Tom's door.

'I'm not going,' he said, as he opened the door. 'I'm not wasting another day at that house.'

However, despite his petitions, he followed her to Darcy Lane and took his place on the fence. She needed company. Since the burglary, she had thought of little else. She coughed and threw a stone towards the bucket.

'Close,' she said. 'I think I've found my talent.'

'Some talent,' he said.

'What's yours?' she asked.

'What?'

'Talent?'

'Patience. And I need it with you.'

Elise's indiscretions had made the local news. She was sat reading from the paper in The Phonebox when an article took her attention. *LOCAL FAMILY BURGLED WHILE AT WEDDING IN SPAIN*, read the headline. *WOMAN TIED TO BED*, read the subhead.

She clutched at the paper and read nervously through the words*, the woman was found the next morning by neighbours* it read, *watches and jewellery taken*.

She read the article and then closed the paper, quickly. She had stayed silent after the burglary, only leaving her house to visit her grandad, work at the shop and visit Darcy Lane. She had not spoken to Jack since the burglary, nor Elijah or Frankie. Jack's advances had troubled her. She had stopped working at the garage too and avoided Elijah's persistent phone calls. She had thought about calling Jack but resisted the urges. Instead, she stayed inside and drank gin.

Tom leant forwards and threw his final stone towards the bucket. It missed and landed on the grass.

Elise smiled. 'You need softer wrists,' she said.

Tom scoffed, 'Sussed it, have you?'

Elise had not told Tom about the burglary or Jack's advances. She could already picture his reaction; shock and dismay. In truth, she had hoped to forget about both Jack and the job.

Despite this, it was not primarily Jack or the job that had been troubling her lately. Instead, it was a bad dream. She wore signs of tiredness on her face, it was clear that she had still not been sleeping well. The dream was about Darcy Lane and her wayward grasp.

The dream was the same each time. It started with her stepping from the bus and walking along the path towards Darcy Lane. She would walk along the path and kick stones. Each time she was happy until she heard voices coming from near the house. She would then rush to the end of the path to see other people living at Darcy Lane. There would be other people swimming in the pond, and other people cutting the grass.

Naturally, she would shriek at the sight. Each time, she saw the same family. She would shout and insist that they leave, but each time they would ignore her. It was like they could not hear her, or that they could hear her and simply did not care. She would shout and scream but the family would not turn, respond, or even lift their heads. She would wake from the dreams in cold sweats. She would then stand from her bed, change her clothes and curl back under the covers in search of proper rest.

'How's Emmett?' asked Tom. 'Is he out of the coma yet?'

'Not yet. Soon, though.'

'Tough bloke, isn't he? Have they got anyone for the attack yet?'

'No, the police still haven't a clue.'

'No arrests, then?'

'No, they're just chasing their tails.'

Tom stood from the fence and started collecting stones from the ground. 'They'll get them,' he said. 'Stay hopeful.'

He placed stones of all sizes into his pockets. He scratched over the ground and kicked through the overgrown grass. He continued until he was satisfied and then retook his place on the fence. He then reached into his pocket and gave a handful of stones to Elise. She put them in her jacket pocket and let her feet dangle freely from the fence. As she did, her phone started to ring. The noise was blunt and intrusive. She left the phone to ring and threw a stone towards the bucket.

'Are you going to get that?' he asked.

Elise shook her head and pulled another stone from her pocket. 'Whatever it is, it can wait,' she said. 'I'm having too much fun beating you.'

She wiped at her eyes and scratched at the skin under her chin. 'I've not been sleeping lately,' she said. 'I'm finding it hard to keep my eyes open.'

Tom threw a stone and glanced towards her. 'Has something been on your mind?' he asked.

Elise shrugged. 'No. Nothing worth mentioning.'

She did want to tell Tom about the burglary. She had contemplated it but eventually thought it unwise. In truth, she was struggling to rid the picture of the woman's face from her mind. The article in the newspaper said that the woman had been *traumatised* by the incident, and that the wounds would be more *mental than physical*. She had tried to think of other things, but the woman's face was persistent. In fact, if her subconscious were not already toiled with the idea of somebody else living at Darcy Lane, she was sure that her dreams would be crowded with pictures of the woman's face.

The article in the newspaper described the culprits as *violent and dangerous to society*. In truth, it was the violence in society that she was trying to escape. She took a stone from her pocket, juggled it between her fingers and threw it towards the bucket.

'That's three,' she said, smiling.

As she sat gloating, her phone started to ring for a second time. Once again, the nearby peace was disturbed by violent rings. She waited until the phone stopped ringing and then stepped from the fence.

'My hands are too cold,' said Tom. 'That's why I'm missing.'

'Put them in your pockets.'

'My pockets are cold too.'

'Moaner.'

'Thanks.'

Tom reached into his jacket pocket. 'Do you want a cigarette?' he asked.

'Do you have some?' she replied.

Tom poured the stones from his hands and pulled two cigarettes from his packet.

'Yeah, I thought I'd get some for when you next dragged me here,' he said. 'I thought it might help pass the time.'

She took a cigarette, lit it, pushed away from the fence, and walked towards the bucket.

She smiled as she looked down at the three stones. 'Domination,' she said. 'Total domination.'

Tom took a drag of his cigarette and looked out towards the house. 'Have you ever wondered who owns it?' he asked.

She turned towards the house. 'No, not really,' she said. 'It's probably just somebody's holiday home.'

He pointed towards the roof. 'It needs some repairs,' he said. 'Water coming through the roof. That wouldn't be much fun on holiday, would it?'

Elise scowled and pointed towards the pond at the back of the house. 'You could swim in the summer,' she said. 'Imagine that, just nipping outside for a swim. It would be great for a holiday.'

'I can't swim,' said Tom.

'Really?'

'My parents never taught me.'

'Well, I can teach you, in summer.'

'No, thanks.'

Elise's phone then started to ring again.

'Will you answer that fucking phone?' he asked. 'That's the third time it's rung. Someone obviously wants to speak to you.'

She took the phone from her pocket and looked at the screen. She hesitated for a moment.

'I don't recognise the number,' she said. 'I'm not answering it. It could be anyone. I'm not in the mood for a stupid call.'

'Answer it,' said Tom. 'Who could it be?'

Elise wilted. She threw her cigarette to the ground and held the phone to her ear. She listened carefully. 'Yeah,' she said. 'This is Elise. Who's this? The hospital?'

Tom watched as her face sunk. She became panicked and started walking back towards the path. As she spoke, her voice became fractured.

'How could that happen?' she asked. 'Is he hurt? Shouldn't someone have been watching his room?'

She turned towards Tom and took the phone from her ear. 'We need to go,' she said. 'Come on.'

She returned the phone to her ear. 'Are the police there?' she asked.

'Okay, I'll be right there,' she continued.

She folded the phone into her pocket and started striding along the path. Tom sprung from the fence and threw his cigarette to the ground.

'What's going on?' he asked. 'Who was it?'

She walked without looking back. Tom ran to catch her up.

'What's the matter?' he asked. 'Has something happened to Emmett?'

She looked from the path and towards the open road. 'When's the next bus?' she asked.

Tom scurried beside her. 'I don't know,' he said. 'There'll be one soon.'

She reached the end of the path and rushed towards the bus stop. 'Where's the fucking bus?'

She turned and kicked at the bus stop. There were tears in her eyes and anger in her voice.

Tom stood with a blank stare. 'Just tell me what's going on,' he said.

She walked out into the middle of the road and looked out in all directions. 'It's too far to run,' she said.

Tom snapped. 'You're fucking scaring me.'

She looked forwards along the road. Her stance was twisted and her attitude bleak.

'That was the hospital,' she said. 'They just caught someone in my grandad's room. Someone was trying to kill him.'

Chapter 16
Mum

Elise sat hunched over a table, cradling a small glass of gin in her hands. The Phonebox was quiet. It was late morning and she sat alone. Her only company being the barman who stood, as usual, reading from a book at the back of the bar. She rolled the glass in her hands. The gin was alluring and warm against her lips. She curled a piece of hair behind her ear and took a long sip. She had not planned on visiting The Phonebox this morning.

As usual, she woke early and stood from bed with the intention of visiting her grandfather at the hospital. However, the news of the second attack had troubled her, so instead, she escaped through the streets and made her way to the bar. She journeyed alone. She had thought about inviting Tom, but in truth, she was in no mood for questions or company. She wanted time to herself, to think, drink, and sulk without interruption.

She arrived at The Phonebox desperate and sweaty. She walked into the bar and quickly ordered a drink. The barman was cautious.

'Are you sure?' he asked. 'It's a little early. How about an orange juice or tea?'

She bit. 'I'll just take the gin, please,' she said.

She took her drink and sat down at the back of the room. As she sat, she noticed the same old man reading from the newspaper at the front of the bar. Perhaps, in her dismay, he was the only constant in her life. He raised an arm and waved towards her. He was wearing an old woollen cap and a pair of glasses. She lifted her glass and waved back. She then finished her drink and returned to the bar to order another. It was clear that she had still not fully accepted the fact that her grandfather had been attacked for a second time.

After her call with the hospital while at Darcy Lane, she caught the next bus and rushed through the streets. She arrived in the intensive care unit to see a swarm of doctors and police officers standing outside her grandfather's room. She tried to push her way into the room but she was stopped by a police officer standing outside the door.

'Who are you?' he asked.

She scowled and pulled away from his grip. 'That's my grandad in there,' she said. 'Now tell me what's happened.'

The police officer stood with his chest between Elise and the door. He spoke with a broad tone: 'One of the nurses found someone in his room playing with the wires, but don't worry, he was stopped in time. There's no harm done.'

'No harm done? Someone's tried to kill him.'

'Yes, but they didn't.'

'Who was watching his room? Shouldn't someone have been watching his room?'

She became animated. She felt heat on her cheeks and tension in her shoulders. 'Where's Dr Violet?' she asked. 'I want to speak to him!'

Elise was restrained by the police officer. She pushed away from him to see Dr Violet walking towards her. He was walking hastily, with his clipboard swinging vigorously by his side.

'Elise,' he said. 'You must be furious.'

She pointed towards her grandfather's room. 'Who was watching him?' she asked. 'How can someone just wander in? I thought he was safe here.'

'He is safe.'

'Did you catch them? The attacker?'

'No, he got away.'

'How the fuck did he get away?'

'Please don't swear.'

'Did you see his face?'

'The nurse didn't get a good look at him, but she's given a description to the police.'

'What was it?'

'Well, an average-sized white male.'

Dr Violet ushered her towards the elongated window outside her grandfather's room.

'I promise you,' he said. 'Nothing else will happen to him. He's safe here.'

The police officer outside Emmett's room then leaned across, he was calm and muscular. 'He's safe here. Don't worry,' he said. 'I'm not leaving this door. Not for a second.'

She ignored his pleas. 'There must be CCTV,' she said. 'It must've got a decent look at him.'

'He had his hood up,' said Dr Violet.

'Why didn't anybody stop him?'

'He was fast. A few of us chased him.'

Dr Violet took her passionately by the arms. 'I promise you,' he said. 'He's safe.'

She smirked and turned away. She had grown tired of promises.

'I'm staying,' she said. 'I'll make sure nothing else happens to him.'

Dr Violet stood nervously. He blushed and looked towards Emmett's stricken figure. 'He is safe,' he repeated. 'But yes, stay. Spend some time with your grandad.'

In the days after, Elise spent much of her time at the hospital. She would arrive early in the morning and only leave to eat and sleep. She was often assured that her grandfather's condition was improving, but in truth, she saw little signs of repair. She spent many hours at the hospital, waiting and standing outside his room.

However, on this morning, the thought of visiting the hospital pained her. She could not spend another morning there – the smell of the walls, the nervous looks – it was all so repulsive. So instead, she made her way to The Phonebox, pressed her lips to the glass, and drank. She stayed at The Phonebox all morning and soon became drunk. She thought and drank, thought and drank. She took a final sip and staggered back to the bar to order another drink.

The barman poured the drink and slid the glass across the bar. 'This is your last one,' he said. 'I'm not having you causing trouble in here. Don't be sick either, our mop's broken.'

She took her drink and gave the barman a drunken thumbs up. She walked back to the table and sat down. As the morning passed, The Phonebox grew in stature. The old man had left and was replaced by a group of men, women, and stray loners. Elise simply lowered her head and kept place in the corner of the room. She sat and slowly drank her final gin. Her lips were cracked and her eyes tired.

She held the glass to her lips and took a short sip. 'Last one,' she mumbled. 'Last gin for me. What a sorry thought.'

She sat regretfully until she saw a familiar figure walk through the doors. It was Elijah. He was pale and out of breath. He noticed her and darted towards her.

'You could answer your phone. I've been looking for you everywhere,' he said. 'Why aren't you at the hospital?'

She glared drunkenly towards him. 'I'm sick of it,' she said. 'Why're you so sweaty?'

'I ran here,' he said. 'From the hospital.'

'For what? A drink? If you're getting one, get me one too. Just don't let the barman see.'

'I came here to see you.'

'All right.'

'It's about Jack. And Emmett. I need to speak to you.'

He pulled up a chair. 'You're going to go mad,' he said.

'Emmett and Jack?' said Elise. 'What about them?'

Elijah paused and lowered his head towards the table. He had started to regain his breath but sweat still formed on his forehead. She noticed his fret and sat up in her chair.

She pushed her glass away and nudged him on the arm. 'What?' she said. 'Tell me now.'

Elijah raised his head, 'It was Jack who attacked Emmett. It was him all along.'

She opened her hand and slapped him on the cheek. She started to brutalise him. He fought with her hands and pushed her back into her chair.

'Stop!' he said. 'Just let me speak.'

Elijah was sodden. He pleaded, and his face wore signs of distress. 'I should've told you sooner,' he said. 'But Jack's been good to me. He gave me somewhere to stay after my mum kicked me out.'

'You promised me!' she said. 'I believed you!'

'I'm sorry.'

'You lied to me. You told me he was with you all night.'

'He left. He thought I was asleep, but I saw him. He came back covered in blood.'

'We have to go to the police.'

'I can't.'

'You have to! Elijah. You have to!'

'Fuck that. I'm leaving.'

'He was attacked again. You could've stopped it, you prick.'

'He promised me that he wouldn't go for him again.'

'Well, he did.'

'And that's why I'm here.'

'We have to go to the police.'

'Go to the police. Tell them everything, but I'm leaving.'

She grabbed him by the hand but he pulled away.

'We have to go to the police together,' she said. 'Tell them everything.'

Elijah stood. 'Leave me alone,' he said. 'I'm gone.'

He tucked his chair under the table and finished Elise's glass of gin.

'How'd it all come to this?' he asked. 'Fucking-hell, how'd this happen?' He sighed, placed the empty glass on the table and started walking back through the bar.

Elise stood and pleaded but he left swiftly.

'Elijah!' she moaned. 'You can't just leave!'

She watched as he pushed his way through the crowd and left through the doors. She fumed, picked up her glass and

119

threw it against the opposite wall. The whole bar turned to look at her.

'Out!' shouted the barman. 'What did I tell you about causing trouble?'

She stormed from the bar and walked to the end of the alleyway.

'Elijah!' she said. 'You lied to me!'

She looked down the street, but Elijah was already gone. She turned and kicked at the old red telephone box.

'Stupid fucking telephone box,' she said. 'He fucking lied to me!'

She walked back inside the alleyway and slumped on the floor. She sat hunched with her head in her hands.

'I'll kill him,' she whispered to herself. 'I'll kill him.'

She pinched at the skin on the back of her hand. The pain was sharp and relaxing. She slapped her knuckles against the ground. Her shoelaces soaked in the dirty water. She thought about her grandad. He had raised her single-handedly from the age of seven. He had tried to fill her with confidence. New shoes for school, school trips, money that he did not have but gave her anyway. And now, he had been attacked by Jack. The more she sat, the shorter her breath became.

She sat until she heard soft sounds coming from the start of the alleyway. She raised her head to see the darkest depths of her imagination. She stood and pushed away from the wall. She looked down at her jeans, cleared away the dirt and smiled as best she could.

Before her, stood, leaning against the old red telephone box, she saw the image of her mother. She was smiling and happy. She still had the same undoubted beauty. She wore a white blouse, with jeans and bare feet. She fixed a piece of daisy blonde hair behind her ear.

She took a half-step forwards, but her mother became scared and stepped back. As she did, the cuts on her blouse became evident. She was bleeding.

'Mum!' she said. 'Mum, it's me!'

She walked towards her mother, but she slipped from view and around the corner. Elise rushed to the end of the alleyway and looked around the corner. She could not see her. She started walking down the street. She looked, but her mother was gone.

'Mum!' she cried. She ran to the end of the street, but there was no sign of her mother.

'Mum, where have you gone?' she asked about her, people stood and watched as she toiled. On the street, tucked into the kerb, sat an empty pint-glass. In her frustration, she picked it up and threw it at the houses across the street. It shattered against the bricks.

'Mum!' she shouted.

'Your mum's not here!' shouted a voice from across the street. 'You're mad!'

She walked back towards The Phonebox and was approached by a young woman.

'Are you okay?' she asked.

She pushed her away. 'Mum, don't disappear,' she said from under her breath. 'Mum, it was Jack who attacked Grandad. Elijah lied to me. Mum!'

'I'm calling the police!' shouted another voice from across the street. 'You've lost it!'

She walked to the side of the street and sat down. Her face was damp, and she was whimpering. From across the street, a man noticed her dismay and started walking towards her.

He approached her and knelt. 'Love, are you okay?' he asked.

She did not respond, so the man sat down on the pavement beside her. 'What's your name?' he asked. 'Maybe I can help?'

The man waited with her until the police arrived. When they did, the officer instantly started shooing away the remaining crowd.

'Go back in your houses,' he said. 'Get on with your day. Have you nothing better to do?'

The officer walked towards her and picked her up from the street.

'It was Jack!' she said. 'It was Jack!'

The officer shook hands with the man who had stayed beside her and then shepherded her back towards the police car.

'Let's get in the car,' he said. 'It's warm in there. We can have a good old talk.'

Around her, people peered and looked on. The officer put her in the back of the car and sat behind the wheel.

'I'm going to take you to the station,' he said. 'What's your name?'

Elise sat and looked out from the car window. As she did, she saw shocked looks and wilted.

'Mum!' she said. 'Mum! It was Jack!'

Chapter 17
Short Laughs

Two Months Later

Elise and Dora sat in the garden at the back of the unit. They sat on the bench, talking, relaxing, and making the most of each other's company. Elise had settled back into the unit without incident. Her mind had started to untangle and her body had adjusted back to the food. There was still a part of her that was disappointed that she could not sustain herself on the outside world. But, for the most part, her return to the unit had been a calming experience.

Despite her growing fondness for the unit, she was still unsure if she would be allowed to stay. After the incident outside The Phonebox, she was taken to the police station. She immediately started to tell the officers about Elijah's confession, and that it was Jack who had attacked her grandfather. The officers smiled and left her in a secure waiting room. One of the officers returned shortly and asked if Elijah would be able to corroborate her story.

She shook her head. 'He's left town,' she said. 'And I don't think he's coming back.'

The officer then left the room again. She could see him talking with other officers outside the door. The officer returned to the room with a friendly smile.

'So,' he said. 'You were recently released from the psychiatric unit, nearly four months ago. Is that right?'

'Yeah.'

'So, we're just going to make a quick call to the unit. It won't take long. Would you like some water while you wait?'

She quickly became furious. 'Why're you not listening?' she asked. 'I've told you about Jack and you're not doing anything. If you don't arrest him, he could do it again.'

The officer started walking from the room. He was flustered and immature.

'Just wait here,' he said. 'Can I get you that water?'

She became desperate and stood from her seat. 'I'd like to confess a crime,' she said. 'The burglary across town, with the woman and the skipping ropes.'

Elise's return to the unit had given her time to think about her time on the outside world. It had now been six months since her initial release and barring her disappointments, she was unsure how to feel. Perhaps, it was the medication dulling her brain or perhaps the last six months had been too complicated to fully understand. She stared at the shelter and thought about the day of her initial release. When she signed her name on the wall and left with the intention of rebuilding her life.

As she thought, she soon became shameful and looked down towards her feet. As she raised her head, her attention was taken by a small bird in a tall tree. She smiled. It was as though the garden had a way of distracting her from her troubles. However, the relief was short lived. She knew that it was not distraction she needed. She knew that if she were ever going to survive on the outside world, she would need to confront her troubles and move towards a resolution.

As she sat, she was still hopeful that she could one day make things work on the outside world. However, she knew that this opportunity would not be forthcoming, so instead, she watched as the bird sat and tried to think of other things.

'Are you nervous about the sentencing?' asked Dora. 'Its next week, isn't it?'

'Yeah, a little.'

'What are you hoping for?'

'Less than five years, and that I can serve my time here.'

'That might be a little optimistic.'

'I don't know. It's hard to say.'

Dora spoke with a sorrowful tone. She was still angry about Elise's return to the unit. She had wanted her to find comfort on the outside world.

'You shouldn't be here,' she said on her return. 'I hoped that I wouldn't see you again.'

Elise was sad to have disappointed Dora. She could see the anguish on her face as they spoke. She knew that she had wasted an opportunity, an opportunity that many of the other patients would have loved to have been afforded.

However, despite Dora's disappointments and her own guilt, she had been welcomed back to the unit. The staff remembered her name and the other patients did not ask questions. She also resumed her sessions with Dr Laghari. They spoke about her time on the outside world and the events that led to her return. Elise tried to speak as freely as possible. They spoke about Jack, Elijah, and Frankie. They spoke about the burglary, and even Darcy Lane.

Dr Laghari told her that she would try to help her stay at the unit. 'This is the best place for you,' she said. 'You're being more honest than last time. That means I can help you.'

Dr Laghari would end each session by reminding her to manage her transition back into the unit. 'Give yourself time,' she would say. 'Returning can sometimes be more difficult than arriving for the first time.'

However, she soon fell back into the routine of the unit. She woke, ate, and took her medication. She slept, talked, and took her medication. Elise admitted that she had stopped taking her medication on the outside world.

Dr Laghari was irritated. 'You've let yourself down,' she said. 'Medication isn't always the answer, but for you, right now, it's essential. You must know yourself better.'

Elise listened. She took her medication and soon her clarity was restored. She started to recognise herself again, as though she was reuniting with an old friend.

'Will they be at the sentencing?' asked Dora.

'Who?'

'The others.'

'Jack and all them?'

'Yeah.'

'No, definitely not.'

Elise sat curling a piece of hair between her fingers. 'Honestly, I hope I never see any of them again.' She then reached into her pocket and pulled out a small tangerine.

Dora looked nervously towards her. 'You're not supposed to take the food,' she said. 'It's against the rules.'

Elise looked over her shoulder. Behind her, staff and patients cleared away the day's lunch.

'They're busy,' she said. 'Anyway, it's only a tangerine.' She started to peel the tangerine. She tore at the skin and left the pieces in a neat pile beside her.

'I want to go with you next week,' said Dora.

'To the sentencing?'

'Yeah.'

'They're not going to let you come. They think you're madder than me.'

'They don't.'

'It's fine. My grandad will come.'

'Is he still not answering your calls?'

'No, it's been a while since I've spoken to him.'

'He'll be sad about all this, won't he?'

'Yeah, he's still got the cases against Jack and the people who burgled his shop to deal with as well.'

'Shit.'

'He's spending too much time at court for a man of his age.'

She tore away the final piece of skin and pulled apart the tangerine. She passed a piece to Dora, who ate it quickly.

'Sweet,' she said.

Elise took a piece and pressed it to her lips. 'I didn't like dinner today,' she said. 'There was something wrong with that bread.'

Dora chuckled. 'The food in prison won't be much better,' she said. 'You should enjoy it here while you can.'

Elise pushed Dora playfully on the arm. 'I might not go to prison,' she said. 'They might let me stay here.'

Dora took another piece of tangerine from Elise's palm. 'They won't let you stay here,' she said. 'You should get that idea out your head.'

She heard honesty in Dora's voice. 'Dr Laghari's trying to help,' she said. 'They might listen to her.'

'Yeah, maybe,' said Dora.

'I don't care, anyway,' replied Elise. 'Whatever happens.'

'What, are you pretending not to care now?'

'Maybe.'

'Well, you shouldn't.'

'Dr Laghari told me that we're the people we pretend to be, sometimes, it's a quote.'

'Who said that?'

'I don't know. Some bloke.'

'Ah. I wonder who he was pretending to be.'

'Not sure – probably a poet. Do you want some tangerine?'

She took the final piece of tangerine and passed it to Dora. 'You can have it,' she said.

Dora took the tangerine, and grinned. 'It's arts and crafts later,' she said. 'That might cheer you up.'

Elise smiled. 'What are you making?' she asked.

'A house,' replied Dora. 'Have you not seen it?'

Elise shook her head. 'No, I got sent out last week. Don't you remember?'

Dora started to tell her about her plans. Elise listened and enjoyed her friend's enthusiasm. Dora described each part of the house in detail; the walls, the roof, and the windows. She told her about the colours the house would be when it was finished and the materials that she would use to make it. She became excited and made the shape of a roof with her hands.

'I don't want it to be too steep,' she said. 'I won't be able to fit the chimney if the roof's too steep.'

Dora continued with her plans until she was disturbed by a loud voice from behind her. She turned to see a member of staff standing by the door to the dining hall.

'It's time to come inside,' he said. 'Come on, I need to lock this door.'

Dora stood. 'You said we could have fifteen minutes!'

127

The man raised his arm and pointed towards the watch on his wrist. 'You've had fifteen minutes,' he said.

Elise stood and gestured towards the man. 'We're coming now,' she said.

'But I was telling you about my house!'

Elise pushed her forwards with her hands. 'You can tell me about it inside,' she said.

Elise and Dora started walking inside. As they did, Elise looked back towards the garden. She had a cruel feeling that this would be her last visit here. 'You never know,' said Dora, 'It might be made out of cardboard now, but maybe I could get myself a nice little house one day. Something with a garden, you know, away from this place.' Elise smiled. She walked away from the garden and along the corridors of the unit, smiling and laughing, with her hands in her pockets.

The End

About the Author

James T. Graham was born on the 28th of December, 1996. Born in London, he was raised in Preston, Lancashire. He started writing in his late teens. *Darcy Lane* is his debut novella.